RIDE
THE
GIANT
WOLF

RIDE THE GIANT WOLF

by Robert C. Wahl

BearManor Fiction

2013

Ride the Giant Wolf

© 2013 Robert C. Wahl

For information, address:

BearManor Fiction
P. O. Box 71426
Albany, GA 31708

bearmanorfiction.com

Cover art by Wendy Wahl-Perry
Author photo by Penny Gentieu
Typesetting and layout by John Teehan

Published in the USA by BearManor Fiction

ISBN—1-59393-388-6
978-1-59393-388-3

For my good brothers, Jan, Phillip,
David, Michael, Douglas,
and mother, Nina Marie

THIS IS A FICTIONALIZED STORY of a young Pawnee warrior whose exploits and those of his tribe come under conflict from within and from warring factions while enduring both famine and drought along the Great Plains, a region which now includes the states of Nebraska, Kansas, and parts of Colorado. The period takes place after the introduction of the horse to the North American continent, yet before the white man had fully explored the west. As history would later attest, it was a time of transition, of radical change occurring between spring and summer, during what the Indians called the *Moon of Making Fat* (June) when buffalo grow lazy from grazing on grass.

Most of all, it is a tale of a boy's life journey into manhood, an indoctrination into the perils of the unknown, across prairie, mountain, and desert, to a place where life was born…

"Listen, Grandfather! Hear the drumming of the partridge? Do you know a story of that?"

"Yes, Grandson. The partridge has a story. The squirrel which sits on yonder limb and scolds our presence has a story. Do you see that tiny insect crawling on the ground? It too has a story. See that great pine with its roots drawing life from the earth, our Mother, and its branches reaching out to the sky, our Father, and that slender blade of grass growing at its roots? Each has its own story. Look! Do you see that tiny speck against the clouds? That is a pelican. See that tiny bird flashing from flower to flower? All have their stories."

– Edward S. Curtis,
photographer, author,
chronicler of the
American Indian,
from Indian Days
of Long Ago

BOOK ONE: FLYING FOX
Worthy of a Pawnee Warrior

Chapter 1

LONG AGO, beside the banks of a quiet river stood a village where cornstalks withered under a hot, glaring sun. Children swam and fished with spears cut from willow branches. Women worked tirelessly, sewing buckskin hides, roasting *ka'wis*, ribs of buffalo over campfires while packs of dogs dozed in the shade, unattended.

No man of fit age was seen anywhere.

Scattered about the bottom of a hill, the earth lodges appeared to be deserted, except for one, prominent for its strategic location and pair of elk antlers hanging above the entrance. Twice the size of any other, the lodge rumbled with a single drumbeat. A second drum soon followed, joined by another, then another, each accompanied by rattles, until there was a great rhythmic pounding of drums and shaking of rattles, and voices chanting a song.

This was *Tuh-parisu*, home of the Pawnee, Village of the Hunters, a tribe of the Wolf Clan which lived along the edge of the High Plains, the prairie lands known as the Long Grass.

Outside the Council Lodge, a young boy stood waiting to enter. When the music stopped, a hand drew the curtain to the entrance open, motioned to the boy, and he entered, humbly presenting himself to the highest members of the tribe. Chieftains, warriors, and priests, dressed in breechcloths, sat around in a circle along the inside walls of the lodge. Besides their age, one thing distinguished the men from the boy—their scalplocks, the *pariki*, Horn of the Bull, a strip of hair fanning down the middle of their skulls. The boy's hair was full and long.

Something about him conveyed a boldness. Perhaps it was his bright, alert eyes, the straightness of his back, the way he carried himself, all of it seemed to suggest a maturity beyond his years. As the chief rose to greet him, the boy stood facing the council leaders, staring through a thick haze of smoke.

"Two Buffalo tells me his son grows restless, wanting to be a man," said the chief to the boy. "Is this true?"

"Yes," said the boy.

Rattles shook and men whispered.

"Why do you wish to go out into the Long Grass?"

"For a long time our hunters have walked the lands of our home, chasing the deer and the buffalo," the boy replied. "They say meat has grown scarce, but where the grass is long, great herds roam. My father tells me no one has hunted there for many summers."

"This is true," said the chief. "And who would you choose to go with you?"

The boy considered his words carefully, summoning all the courage he had. "I would choose no one. I would go alone."

"Alone?"

There were quick, darting looks of surprise. Chatter. Even laughter.

"You would take no one? No dogs to carry the meat home?"

"None will be needed. I will carry the cloak and part of the meat from the animal I wish to kill."

The Council grumbled in protest while rattles trembled like a nest of angry snakes. It was one thing to be courageous, another to be rash, especially when danger lurked everywhere, under every bush, tree, and blade of grass in the prairie.

The chief held up his hands and everyone grew quiet. "But what of the rest of the meat?" he asked. "Did Two Buffalo raise a fool who would leave it to the scavengers?"

"No," answered the boy, humbly. "I wish to share the meat with the *Nabu'rac.**"

Mutterings of confusion swept through the lodge.

"Share in what way?" asked the chief.

The boy explained, "We Pawnee need meat. This I know. But by-sharing with the *Nabu'rac*, the trail will be blessed wherever a Pawnee happens to go."

---

*animal gods

"And how will you stop the scavengers from stealing from the *Nabu'rac?*"

"By burning what I do not keep and letting the wind carry the ashes in all four directions, to the far lodges where the *Nabu'rac* live."

Again, the men of the Council whispered, but this time in admiration.

"But, alone, you may get lost or hurt," the chief warned, "trampled by a bull buffalo, attacked by a Comanche or Sioux. What do you say of this?"

After looking at the faces around the lodge, the boy turned to the chief and said, "But I will not be alone. I have my grandfather to watch over me, his father, and his father before him, and all the others who have gone before us."

The chief thought for a moment and replied, "You speak well for one so young." To the Council, he added, "Is there anyone here who would deny Flying Fox his quest for manhood?"

No one spoke. Consent was given in silence.

After consulting with the Council leaders, the chief nodded. "Go then," he said. "You may leave at the next Morning Star. But choose your weapons wisely. Pray to the *Nabu'rac* for guidance, for these are bad times. I do not remember when we have had so little rain. The animals are thirsty. They have taken to the trail of *awahi**. If Flying Fox acts as well as he speaks, the *Nabu'rac* may look favorably upon him."

He waved the boy away.

Flying Fox had long awaited this moment of his life. Now his dream of becoming a warrior had come. To the Council he nodded, showing no emotion. As he quietly turned to leave, rattles shook and drums pounded.

Once outside, he could barely contain himself. He wanted to release his joyous spirit, run through the village, and let everyone know the quest for his dream had been granted. But he knew the first lesson a warrior must practice was restraint until he succeeded in whatever test, battle, or feat he was set to do. So he suppressed the urge and went to the top of a hill to sit. He sat for a long, long time, praying and singing, while the clouds passed from above and stars filled the void in the

---

* here and there

moon-less sky. Posed on his knees, hands gesturing upward, he called to the *Nabu'rac—*

"Flying Fox is here, on the hill. Do you see him, *Nabu'rac*? What a good day tomorrow will bring if you offer him one of your own. If not for Flying Fox, do it for his mother and father so they can say their son is now a man."

He chanted and prayed all through the night, not knowing his father watched and listened from the family lodge. In all of his years Two Buffalo had never heard of anyone venturing out into the Long Grass alone and surviving for more than a day or two at most, not on his own free will. But his son was unlike any boy or man of the *Wolf Pa'ni*.

Flying Fox was prepared to explore a new world—a world full of change, of mysterious winds blowing across the sun-scorched plains, of the great trampling herds of *taraha*, of far-reaching lands, and an enemy he would soon come to know.

Chapter 2

BY THE TIME THE DOGS HOWLED, waking the Pawnees from sleep, Flying Fox was far from the familiar hills surrounding his village. Armed with a bow, arrows, knife, snares, and rope, he was properly equipped for hunting, yet not overly burdened for the journey. He took a pouch, a sacred bundle his father gave him. In it, he carried wolf teeth to remind him to hunt only during times of hunger, hawk feathers which gave him courage, and implements to make a fire.

As he went, he remembered many of the things Two Buffalo had taught him. "When traveling," his father said, "always keep out of sight as best you can. Because you cannot see something does not mean it is not there. You never know who or what may be watching you." Concerning the safer aspects of travel, Two Buffalo advised, "When approaching a hill, creep along the ravine. In the grass, stay to the tallest parts. Where there are trees, walk among the thickest stands. When you come to a river, do not tread along the bank unless you wish to meet your enemy."

So Flying Fox did just that. He followed the river for a while, then cut through the plains among the Long Grass, and, as he was doing now, crept toward a hill by way of a ravine. Quietly, he circled the high ground until he reached the top. From there, he could see far across the parched and yellowed flats. Beyond the flights of many arrows, a bull elk sipped water from a silvery pond. Just before the elk loped away, he put an imaginary arrow in his bow and aimed.

The elk, however, was too far away to pursue, so he walked down to the pond to find a stagnant pool of water, thick and clogged with mud. Fish bones lined the rim of the dusty basin where the water level had receded during the drought. Around the bank he placed two snares, hoping a rabbit or small beaver might wander in to drink. Throughout the afternoon he waited downwind in the brush, enduring the heat of the sun and pestering ants, which crawled over his skin. Aside from an occasional bird, the only creature he saw was a snake, as plump as his arm. It stopped a few feet away, hissed, flicked its tongue at him, shook its tail loudly, then slithered into the underbrush with surprising swiftness. From the diamond-shaped markings on its skin, he knew it was a rattlesnake, the most venomous of all snakes, the bite of which could kill.

At nightfall, hungry and restless from inactivity, Flying Fox made a grassfire near the water's edge, then tied one end of a rope to a rock and the other end to the shaft of an arrow. "I have seen the Ponca use fire as bait to attract fish," his father once said, "and a roped arrow to bring the catch in."

Indeed, Two Buffalo was right. With one shot, his son had food thrashing at the tip of the noosed arrow. After pulling it in, he quickly cooked and ate the meaty flesh, and once again, following his father's wise counsel, moved on.

"Whenever you make camp," Two Buffalo cautioned, "always leave the place where you enter by day and find another when it is dark. That way, if your enemy sees where first you went and attacks at night, no one is there to kill."

A short distance away, Flying Fox found a safe place to sleep. He nestled down in the grass, clutching his knife, and dreamed of a buffalo slain by courage and skill.

At sunrise, he faced the grim prospect of turning the imagined into fact. Perched nearby, a blue bird whistled, scolding him for sleeping so much. He awoke with a start, rubbed his sleepy eyes, and proceeded west in the hopes of seeing signs of buffalo or elk. Slowly, the soft, rolling hills became more pronounced. By mid-morning, a gust of wind whipped through the grass, blowing up dust so thick he could barely see, let alone for any great distance. All he could do was concentrate on the path ahead and suffer through it as best he could.

Eventually, as the day wore on, it grew warmer. The wind began to die, and new set of problems arose: Insects. Fields and fields of them.

Whenever he took a step, there was a great buzzing and scattering of bugs flitting every which way at once. Flies, mosquitoes, grasshoppers, locusts, cicadas came flying at him en mass and got into his hair, his eyes, his clothing, while crawling over every inch of his sweat-soaked body.

At times he thought he was under attack. Fighting them was useless. Escape, impossible. For every annoying insect he would swat, three or four would attach themselves to him. All he could do was shield his eyes, endure a rash of stings and bites, and move on. Fortunately, like the windstorm preceding it, the swarm of insects soon passed.

Realizing peril rested in the most innocent looking places, he traveled cautiously, sometimes running, sometimes walking, often hiding to see if he were being followed.

Luckily, he was not.

Solitude, his father once told him, was something every man should experience—whether in the wild, pursuing a dream or vision, or finding his way in places unfamiliar or dangerous.

Flying Fox did not fear being alone. In many ways he celebrated it. To him it was a necessary step in the process of becoming a man. Whatever he chose to do, he did. Like eating. Foraging had become second nature to him. Wild onions, nuts, weeds, buckthorn, chokecherry, jimson, potato, wild plum. He knew if he looked hard enough, he could find food just about anywhere. If one part of a plant was not edible, in all probability a leaf, stem, or root was.

Among a patch of blueberries he paused to eat when he heard a high-pitched call of a bird twice the size of any bird he had ever seen. It glided effortlessly with outstretched wings and white-tipped tail. Upon its balding head was a crown of white. Larger than a hawk, much larger than a raven, he had never seen such a magnificent bird as it swooped gracefully in total command of the air. Just as quickly as it appeared, as if by magic, it was gone. Flying Fox searched the sky long after it vanished, the echo of the Giant-Winged Bird lingering, a memory he would not soon forget.

For half of the day he explored the wilderness without further incident until at last he saw, rising above the grass, what looked like a curved set of pointed branches. As any experienced hunter would know, these were not branches. They moved. And by the size and number of horns comprised in the antlers, he realized it had to be an exceptionally large stag as well.

Always alert for predators, the buck lifted its head, chewing on a mouthful of weeds, and stared across the prairie. At the same time Flying Fox crouched into the surrounding grass. To lure the animal closer, he blew on a reed, imitating the cry of a fawn, then listened.

The air barely stirred with a whisper. Again, he blew on the reed, waited, and blew once more to entice it closer still. The grass rustled as he took hold of his bow, anticipating the moment.

Instead of the buck, a curious young deer poked its nose through the underbrush, almost nudging the tip of the arrow. He could not shoot.

The startled fawn was too young to kill. Like him, it was just learning how to survive. As he lowered his bow, it ran off, as did the buck.

Quietly, he followed. A path was made where they ran, the growth matted, pushed aside, the earth soft, yielding to the cloven hoof, so he had no trouble tracking the animals. Up and down hills and through ravines he trotted, not knowing the extent of the chase, or how long it would take. About the time he began to tire, the distance from one track to the next shortened. Which meant they were no longer running.

He took advantage of it by catching his breath. As he did, he looked up. High above a gentle-sloping hill, he saw buzzards circling. He rushed ahead to find flies, ants, and insects crawling over the remains of a doe. Her flesh has been torn cleanly, viciously from the bones. Chunks of skeleton lay broken, ravaged by eaters who evidently had gone mad. The area was trampled, covered in blood still warm from the kill. He studied the other tracks. Unlike those of a deer's whose hoof was oval, having four distinct parts, these tracks were made by paws—four narrow toes in front, one larger, wider imprint in back.

Skiri!

Wolves!

When hungry, a roaming pack of wolves, will attack almost anything. Sometimes even men. Knowing he was in danger, Flying Fox climbed the nearest tree and scanned the Long Grass from one end to the other.

Neither deer nor wolf were anywhere in sight.

But the cautious words of his father served as a reminder: "Because you cannot see something does not mean it is not there."

While the buzzards hovered above, waiting to gorge themselves on the doe, he slid down from the tree and walked to the next hill. Spreading apart the high grass with his bow, he looked out across the prairie where a herd of buffalo was grazing lazily under the hot sun.

He counted forty in all, heads bent low, tails tossing contentedly as they ate. Calves clung to their mothers' sides, some of them nursing. As usual, whenever a herd of buffalo grazed, bulls flanked the perimeters for protection.

His heart leapt excitedly at the prospect of making a kill, until he noticed the smoke. Five or six patches curled up toward the sky, enclosing the herd on three sides. Then he saw fire. Movements in the grass.

Comanches!

A hunting party had the wind at their backs. The buffalo were caught between the hunting party and a ridge skirting a river. Suddenly, the Comanches cast their torches aside and screamed like wounded hawks, waving their arms, jumping up and down. The fires spit up barriers of flame which flared and ran together through the dry brush. Fed by wind and grass, the flames spread, burning in everwidening rows amid heavy, swirling clouds of smoke. The buffalo panicked, stampeding in confusion, leaving only one direction in which they could escape: away from the smoke. They stopped at the top of the ridge, pushing, shoving, jostling near the edge. The fires closed around them crackling unbearably hot, singeing hide, scorching flesh. The herd shrieked and bellowed as they slipped over the edge, splashing into water—water so shallow he could hear bones snapping as they struck bottom where a shoal of rocks lay just beneath the surface. One after another, the animals tumbled over the ledge. Cows, bulls, calves. Legs flailing. Crushing the ones beneath them. Crashing into a pile of thrashing bodies below.

The surviving buffalo swam as best they could, knowing somehow that safety lay on the opposite bank. As soon as they reached it, another hunting party with bows and arrows rushed forward to attack. Half of the herd floated downriver, heads barely above water, struggling, gulping for air, only to sink and disappear into the currents beneath where they quietly choked and drowned. The rest made it ashore, slipping through mud, over layers of rock. They stumbled across sand bars, staggered up the steep embankments, grunting in terror while trampling two calves underfoot in a desperate attempt to stay alive. At the same time, the bowmen descended, shooting their arrows. One by one, the targets fell, knees buckling, bodies heaving on the ground, some of them having as many as five or six arrows stuck in their guts, necks, and flanks.

From both sides of the river, hunters converged, whooping and hollering as they plunged their spears into the few remaining creatures still alive. There was a last great outcry from the beasts and an even louder outcry from the Comanches. In the meantime, the drag bearers and drag dogs brought poles around for the stowing and transporting of the carcasses homeward before the blood-letting and butchering commenced.

As Flying Fox watched from the hill, he could feel his emotions raging like the fires burning below. He had never seen a hunt of this kind. To him, the method employed in the kill was wrong. A direct kill, using a bow and arrow or a spear, caused no harm outside of what was intended to do. But a fire? With so little rain, there was nothing to prevent it from spreading. Which led to one terrifying and inescapable conclusion. The entire plains, every inhabitant, man and animal, were now in danger, including those who lived in his village.

And what of the *Nabu'rac*, the gods and spirits? What would they say or do? Would they think the Pawnees were responsible and vent their wrath on the innocent and good?

A great harm the Comanches had done, this much he knew. He considered them an vile, evil people who had no regard for *Earth Mother*, the animals they killed, or the *Nabu'rac*.

And indeed, just as he feared, the wind changed direction and blew towards him. The fire widened, flicked up in great whirling gusts, consuming huge tracts of grass and brush, leaving a burnt swath of blackness in its path. He watched until he could stand the heat no more. The grass fumed, chasing after him like thousands of fiery beasts. The smoke haunted, billowing upward with clouds of ash and soot like hordes of angry ghosts.

The fire was close enough he could feel the heat. And closing fast. He had to run. Escape. Now! So he fled, retreating down the hill. Each blade of grass seemed to slow him down, to pull at him, to want to trap him like an animal in a snare. He ran faster and faster, seeming always slower, the pace ever harder. Whether leading into danger or not, he did not care. Through the vastness of the prairie he dashed, never stopping, never looking back, never knowing if he could escape what was truly becoming a Land of Fire.

For as long as there was sun in the sky he ran. He ran until his legs cramped, sides ached, and feet bled, the wear of rock and weed tearing through his moccasins. He ran until his mouth was parched, until he had sweated every bit of sweat from his skin and it lay dried, a sheet of gritty salt, over his entire body. He ran beyond the point of numbness, beyond hurt, beyond fatigue, until he could run no more.

At dusk, the horizon blazed crimson, with gray shadowy figures of smoke rising toward the stars. He was now the hunted. No weapon could offer protection. He was as helpless as all the other animals trembling in the night. He could hear hoof beats, tiny creatures scurrying through the grass, predators and prey alike in mass retreat, swarming over the drought-ridden expanse. From the antelope to the fox, from the rattlesnake to the long-tailed prairie mouse, they were trying to do as he, only with more abandon. In the end, there was little he could do. He had to rest. And so he rested, not wanting to sleep, but sleep he did.

Once he woke up, he thought he had dreamed, but the smell of smoke and fiery devastation proved otherwise, so onward he pushed, weary and terribly sore while night still prevailed. Again, there was no slackening of pace, no pausing to relax. He ran as hard and fast and for as long as his legs could carry him, widening the distance between him and the dreaded Comanche fire. He entered the village the next day without a skin of buffalo or cloak of elk. Just word of what approached was all he had.

As he told his father of the fire, he realized his chance of becoming a warrior had been lost. He did not remember much after that, except for the shouting and yelling and people hurrying every which way at once. Mostly he remembered how tired he was—how tired and racked with pain. For almost two full days he had run. His legs were completely spent, as weak and lame as any old man's who hobbled to his grave, and that is how he made it home—a boy hobbling to his family's lodge.

His mother, Musk Raven, laid him down on a bed of pelts. Once again he dreamed, this time of the faceless Comanches and the ruin they had wrought. He dreamed of buffalo, of *taraha*, stampeding with hoofs aflame and heads of smoke and the land burning wherever they went. Finally, the trample faded into darkness where the *Nabu'rac* lodged and he fell into a complete and exhausted sleep.

When he opened his eyes, he saw the smiling faces of his mother and father, and the chief leaning over him.

"Good. You are rested," said the chief. "Because of you the fire was put out in time. You cannot wear that honor like a cloak or feed your mother when she is hungry. But a boy can become a man in other ways. Come. The Council awaits its youngest brave."

*   *   *

Later that evening, while the sun was setting, Flying Fox sat atop the hill, wearing a string of feathers in his scalplock. Not just a symbol of a warrior, the hair, as well as the headdress, were worthy of the highest chieftain.

He stared at the contrast between the blackened fields surrounding the village and uncharred stalks of corn where a ditch was dug and the fire died.

He wondered.

The sky uttered thunder and it began to rain.

BOOK TWO: WOLF RIDER
The Vision Quest

Chapter 3

*"Here is the story of my footsteps
on many trails…"*

– Black Elk,
from *Black Elk Speaks*

IT WAS NOW *Moon of the Whispering Locust* (July) and for one brief night there was rain, followed by thirty days of drought.

Life in the Pawnee village was growing desperate. Cornstalks stood wilted in the field, dead. Beans and squash hung unpicked from vines, never having lived long enough to ripen. The ground beneath was as hard as rock, caked by the sun, the river so shallow a child could wade from bank to bank and never go deeper than his waist. As the water level declined, so declined the amount of fish caught. To make matters worse, the herds of buffalo, elk, and deer had forsaken the fire-ravaged lands for pastures elsewhere.

Aside from food, animals provided the basic ingredients needed to sustain life. Of prime importance was the buffalo. Skins were made into boat covers, tepees, clothing, and bags; sinew into thread, bowstrings, and fiber for ropes. Hair was woven into ornaments, belts, and tied into brushes for grooming. Tools were crafted from bones while skulls were bleached, used as decorations around the lodges, during ceremonies, and at burial sites. Sustenance, however, was the buffalo's main purpose. Without it, hunger or famine resulted. As many of the older Pawnees could attest, never before had anyone experienced such a dry summer.

No one felt more helpless than the Rainmaker. Every day he would place a prayer stick upon a bundle of grass and ask Earth Mother and Sky Father to make a treaty between them. Then, after sprinkling dust all around—a gesture of falling rain—he would chant, dance, and sing, and shake his storm rattles from sunup to sundown, day after day, and crawl into a sweat lodge at night and remain there until morning in the hope of purifying himself, of making himself deserving in the eyes of the storm gods. But, unfortunately, the rain never came.

With all these signs of displeasure—from the *Nabu'rac, Opirikut,** Earth Mother, and Sky Father—the Council decided it was time to find a new home where food was plentiful. The priests and shamans read it in the stars, the chiefs saw it in their dream-visions, and the warriors agreed since they had hunted with little or no success. Not known for their nomadic ways, this was a drastic undertaking for the Pawnees, as was the direction chosen.

In one of his more impassioned speeches, the chief declared, "Across the Long Grass we shall travel, into the High Country, Land of the Tall Pines," meaning, far from their neighboring tribes—the Kiowa, Wichita, and Caddoan brother and sisters—where few of their kind had gone.

So a Long March was decreed and the next day a feast was prepared with what little food they had. Hunters were sent out to bring back meat—if not buffalo, at least rabbit—while a group of children, led by Flying Fox, went out into the river to catch trout.

When asked why they were taking no nets, he smiled and replied, "All we need is our hands and a good stick."

Borrowing an idea from the beaver, they found a place downriver where the water was no deeper than their waists. Willow branches were cut and wedged among some rocks to form a trap, much like a dam. Currents could flow through it, but fish could not pass. Once the trap was set, the children stood an arm's length from each other, occupying one side of the river. After spotting a fish, they splashed and stirred the water vigorously, forcing the fish to swim to the opposite bank. Only a sharp stick was needed to do the rest. By mid-afternoon, to everyone's amazement, each child was carrying an armful of fish back to the village.

---

* deity of fertility and agriculture

When darkness came, there was a big celebration. Campfires blazed with trout and duck and rabbit skewered on sticks. Furious was the dancing as warriors and *parisa* told stories of former battles and animals they had hunted. Many of them used their hands to form words and recite feats of daring. One story led to another, followed by more dancing, and into the night the celebration continued.

Among the favorites was an old tale told by the Rainmaker. "Back when the world was young," he said, "there was no thunder. Animals had no shirts or hides or hair and walked around like men. Sky Father, they say, lived among the people and he, too, looked like a man.

"For many days and nights there was no rain. If lightning struck, it brought fire to the grass and trees.

"One day, Sky Father walked up to Coyote and said, 'Bring me a hollow piece of log and I will change the world, make it a better place.'

So Coyote did. He brought a hollow piece of log.

"Then Sky Father walked up to Fox and said, 'Bring me a skin of leather, one that is good and strong, and I will change the world, make it a better place.' So Fox did. He brought a piece of leather, one that was good and strong.

"Then Sky Father walked up to Beaver and said, 'Bring me a knot of wood, one I can hold in my hand, and I will change the world, make it a better place.' So Beaver did. He brought a knot of wood, one that Sky Father could hold in his hand.

"Once everything was gathered, he stretched the skin of leather over the hollow piece of log and struck it with the knot of wood, making a loud noise.

"'What is that?'" the people asked.

"'This is a drum,' replied Sky Father. He pointed at the sky and said, 'I will place it up there, where the clouds are dark, and when you hear it again, you will know it as *thunder.*'

"'And what is thunder?' someone asked.

"'Thunder is a warning,' he said. 'From this day forward…and all the days and nights to come, when there is a storm, there will be thunder, and when you hear it, you will know that rain is coming.'"

Everybody smiled as drums began to pound. Long into the night they sang and danced. But, still, the rain did not come.

Early the next morning, the earth lodges were stripped bare, the fires quieted, and everyone assembled in the center of the village where poles were lashed to drag dogs and all the possessions were packed for the journey. The place called *Tuh-parisu*, Village of the Hunters, was left to the wind ghosts. The shamans spoke of a land near the mountains, the Shiny Mountains, where herds of buffalo grazed, the earth was fertile for farming, and water was in great supply. The people lifted their hearts in song and the weeping memory of *Tuh-parisu* was forgotten.

The tribe began its march by following the Snake River, called that because it snaked its way down from the Shiny Mountains. At the head of the procession, chieftains and warriors carried their lances, priests and shamans their long ceremonial staffs, to fend off evil should it come their way. Behind them walked their families, squaws and children who flogged grass switches at the drag dogs to keep them in line.

An advance party of Trail Watchers scouted ahead in search of food. Only the ablest of hunters were chosen because they had to protect or warn against possible attack by an enemy war party. Among those given that honor and responsibility was Flying Fox. He could faintly hear the song of his people behind him while the wind blew up dust thick and dark as clouds when rain falls.

Whenever he happened upon anything worth eating—roots, berries, or a nest of eggs—he would stuff them in a buffalo bladder. The bladder bulged until he could fill it no more. Using a stick, he forced six fat gophers out of their holes and into his snares, then walked among the brush and shot several rabbits with his bow and arrow. By the time the tribal campfires signaled all scouts to return, he had enough food to feed three families.

When he entered camp, so heavy was the load he carried, the poles from which they hung almost snapped. A proud father Two Buffalo was. So proud, he invited the chief, his family, and many others to feast on gopher tallow. While the meat was cooking, men gathered around the campfire to talk of the journey and the lands they hoped to find.

The chief described how the Shiny Mountains were *"feathered with trees."* He claimed to have many dream-visions of great beauty there— *"Of rivers tumbling off cliffs. And snows that never melted."*

Priests and warriors said they, too, had visions of a land where *"the wind rattled through the trees,"* the wolf had a coat the color of *"dark gray smoke,"* and the piercing cry of a bird whose wingspan *"was wide as a man was tall"* was heard.

"I have seen this bird you speak of," said Flying Fox.

A hush fell. Everyone urged him to go on.

"It flew as fast as the wind," he said, "was dark as night, with feathers of white at the tips of its wings and tail, and soared so high it vanished like a ghost. Where it was going, I do not know, but I am glad it did not come near me because it had very big claws and a voice that cut through the sky like a singing arrow."

"I have heard many people talk of this bird," replied the chief. "From what I am told it lives mostly in the mountains. The Ute and Shoshone call it an eagle."

There was much talk after that, about visions and dreams and what they mean to a young man. Two Buffalo remarked to everyone that he expected great things of his son and suggested Flying Fox go on a vision quest one day. "When he is older," he said. "When he is ready."

The chief agreed, saying, "Perhaps it is wise to wait. Once we have settled after our Long March, he may see his future…and perhaps ours, too, in the new land."

Since a vision quest was considered an honor befitting a man, the mere mention of it set fire to Flying Fox's blood. "Father," he asked, "now that I am a warrior, cannot I choose when I go?"

Two Buffalo rubbed his chin in thought. "Yes," he answered, "you may choose."

"Then say a prayer for me, for tomorrow I go."

"But this is a dangerous time," said Two Buffalo. "You will be weak, in no condition to travel alone."

"But the spirits are here, Father," said Flying Fox, "not where we are going."

Two Buffalo sat, brooding, with a look of concern on his face. From the campfire he broke off a leg of rabbit and passed it to his son. "Eat," he said. "Tonight you need nourishment, for tomorrow you must fast."

So Flying Fox ate the leg of rabbit. When he was finished eating, Two Buffalo took him to the edge of camp. "Let me tell you of a place," he said "and what you must do to have a vision."

There, by a ridge, overlooking the Snake River, they shared a pipe. They smoked to the earth, the sky, and four winds—first, to the west where the Thunder Beings Live; then to the north where the Great Wind Blows; next, to the east where the Sun Rises; and finally to the south where the Summer Comes—and talked late into the night, watching the stars.

Chapter 4

*"A man can tell by the size and depth of
the tracks much about his quarry..."*

– Black Elk,
from *Black Elk Speaks*

At daybreak, from atop the crest of a hill, Flying Fox watched his people resume their march through the prairie. Although he was alone, he now had his father's wise counsel from the night before to give him support. Supplied with only a knife and two prayer sticks, he set out in the direction they had come. He carried no other weapons or food, for he depended upon the gods and spirits to guide him safely through it. He knew the risk he was taking, but quickly put the thought out of his mind because nothing was to interfere with his purpose: first, to seek an abode of spirits, then to fast for several days, proving his worthiness. Afterwards, the spirits might take pity on him and provide what he needed.

Heading east, he walked all morning and all afternoon until the first eye of Sky Father glared fiery orange on the horizon. He came to a ridge where several boulders rose above the ground seven to ten feet high. Here, legend claimed, was a place where four great Pawnee chiefs once lived. When the chiefs died, the earth lodges turned to stone, capturing their powerful spirits. Based on what his father had told him, this seemed the perfect spot to carry out his vision quest.

"Remember to face the sun," Two Buffalo suggested. "Watch it until it is gone and the stars look down upon you. Always keep a fire burning, to keep the wolves away."

To make a fire, he piled shredded bark and dry grass upon a rock and twirled a small branch between his palms, pressing downward, creating friction, then smoke, then placed a layer of twigs over the dry grass until flames began to flicker. Huddled between the fire and the boulder, he held the prayer sticks across his chest and waited until the moon, the second watchful eye of Sky Father, crept into the sky. When it was directly overhead, he chanted and prayed to the ghost-spirits of the four great chiefs.

"It is best to call them by name," Two Buffalo explained. "And though you will become weak, in your weakness they will see that you are strong. A good heart and noble spirit are what you must show."

So Flying Fox spoke each of their names and said to the most powerful of the chiefs, "I have come to your lodge, Ouray, a man just made. The *Nabu'rac* and *Opirikut* have given us little to eat, so it is time to make a new home. We go seeking their blessing and I have come to seek yours. I am still a boy in many ways. My eyes do not see like a man's. I have no wife, no family to feed. I am not yet as wise as the older ones. But I may grow wiser if you fill my eyes with a vision. I am here sitting by your lodge, Ouray. Can you see where Flying Fox sits?"

Modesty was at the heart of all prayer. He spoke of his past humbly, citing the mistakes he made as a child and also as a man, so he could be judged for who he was, as well as what he had done.

After dusk, there were noises all around him—the scuffle of feet, the chitter of birds, of squirrels, the rustle of grass as animals wandered past the campfire. He could see them by the glow of their eyes, reflecting off the fire. An owl cried, "*A-hoo! A-hoo!*" A pack of wolves crept by, but were heard a little while later howling in the distant hills. The fear of attack always existed no matter how bright and how hot the fire, yet he knew he could not think of only himself.

"Think of visions, of voices and of songs," Two Buffalo told him.

Finally, coyotes called, but he did not hear them. The night became cold, but he did not feel it. He was totally obsessed with winning the trust of those who slept in the Stone Lodges, especially Ouray.

Throughout the night and the next day he did not stray from his purpose. Nor did he eat, sleep, drink, or move from his position. At times he felt drowsy. His stomach fought hunger. His legs grew numb from the lack of movement. But he had denied himself so much and had done it with such force of will he overcame the discomfort. Two Buffalo told him the more miserable his condition, the more likely the ghost-spirits would come to his aid. So he took a loose rock and struck his left hand with it. Pain shot up his arm. Suddenly, he was aware of every ache, every cramp, all he had subjected to his body.

As night wore on, he weakened more and more. The pain spread to his legs, arms, and back. He surrendered to the cold. His mouth went dry. His eyes began to blur. Dizzy from the lack of sleep and badly in need of water, he suffered in every respect, time and again pushing himself to the limits of endurance, then finding new strength from places he knew not where, willing his body to withstand even more. In spite of it all, he chanted continuously, softly summoning the ghost-spirits to take pity on him.

Still, he saw nothing, only the dark of night.

At first light, he climbed atop the largest boulder and called to the spirits again, to seek their assistance while words from his father filled his head—

"Do not think of your mother, or of me, or of food or water. Let your thoughts be of nothing. Follow the sun as it drifts across the sky and fades into darkness. Perhaps on the second night you will grow weaker and fall down as if dead and hear voices. And you will see something that looks like a man but is not a man. He will sing you a song—a song you must keep in your heart. And if, after the second night, still no voices come to you, you will sit for another night and another day and watch the sun and moon as they come and go again, then after all of this, surely the spirit voices will talk to you."

Once again, Flying Fox did everything as before, only with a sense of urgency. The misery he felt earlier returned with a vengeance. His knees and back became sore. Hunger gnawed at his belly. Thirst came to his lips. And there were moments when he believed he could do no more, had spent himself physically as well as emotionally. He was so exhausted he could barely sit up straight or keep his thoughts focused on what he was trying to do. His eyes wanted to close, but the pain was the only thing that kept him awake. Pain from the heat of the sun. Pain from sitting in one place too long. Deprivation.

Still he heard no voices, no songs.

Now and again he would have lapses, moments of drowsiness and uncertainty where he hardly saw anything at all. He had to rub his eyes to make himself see. Whether they were hallucinations or mirages, he did not know. His mind would wander. His eyes would play tricks on him, yet he always returned to a sort of state of grace where he was rational and clear-headed. He often reeled and swayed without realizing it and images drifted through his head without the ability to distinguish if it was a dream or not. Pain came and went, as did numbness, especially in his legs and feet where the blood did not flow.

Once in a while a cold wind blew. Chills ran deep into his bones. His perceptions would falter and he would fall into oblivion, only to reemerge a new man, invigorated by the sheer force of his will, even though he was unaware of what was at work, or why. His senses—those of hearing, touch, sight, and feel—became blunted one moment and acute the next. He always seemed to be on the verge of one extreme or another. Yet no matter how hard he tried, he was never able to attain that state of mind between consciousness and sleep where imaginings seemed real and reality a perception.

In an act of desperation he reached for his knife. He recalled several stories about Vision Seekers who resorted to torture and self mutilation when all else failed. In one case, he knew of a warrior who held his hand over a fire until the skin was scorched. In another, a well-respected priest named Medicine Crow sliced open the skin along his belly and allowed the cut to bleed. Eventually, after having lost so much blood, he grew weaker and weaker, until late one summer evening, sitting alone in a drenching rain storm, weak, enfeebled, in need of sleep, he had a vision.

Having tried everything else, Flying Fox had no recourse. Holding his left hand over a rock, he slowly brought the knife down until the blade touched the little finger. With the weight of his body leaning forward, brow sweating, hands shaking, he was about to sever the little finger when he heard a cry from a bird above. He looked up and saw something moving very fast...the blur of a winged shadow as it flew past the boulder. He listened. There was a flutter of wings, a rustle in the underbrush, followed by a loud cry. With a powerful leap, the bird flew off, clutching its prey in its claws.

Was this a sign? Were the *Nabu'rac* displeased with him? Would it make him any more of a man if he had one less finger?

Somehow he could not bring himself to do it. He heard the blade of the knife clatter against rock as it slipped from his hand. Delirious, having lost all sensation in his hands and feet, he began to tremble and sway. With both arms raised, he beseeched Ouray and the *Na-bu'rac* to grant him a vision. He sang all day, explaining that he had not eaten for two moons, nor drank of water, nor slept. He was waiting—waiting for someone to come and end his misery.

And, still, he saw nothing.

At dusk, a great wind blew from the west, where the Wind is Born and the White Corn Maiden Sings…where the Big Monster swallowed all the water and the Monster Slayer honed his knife from flint and slew the Big Monster, releasing all the water to the lakes and rivers. As night fell, deep in Buffalo Country, there came a noise. The moment he heard it he forgot about everything else. He forgot about the pain, the hunger, the thirst, the numbness in his legs. A weight seemed to be lifted from his shoulders as he tried to concentrate on the sound.

Somewhere in the distance, growing louder by the moment, there was a great drumming of hoofs, almost as if the earth were shaking. He was vaguely aware of movement, of animals, sleek and long-bodied, trampling stride for stride in a herd.

Battling to stay awake, he slumped to his knees and through red, watery eyes he saw—

A great cloud of dust drifting closer and closer.

It drifted up from the bases of the Stone Lodges and seemed to hover in the air. Deep inside the cloud there was smoke, and from the smoke *four figures began to emerge, their bodies floating like images upon the water.*

Chieftains they were. Spirits. That much he knew—giant in size…

… and not in the likeness of men. Their faces were covered in hair and bore a likeness similar to wolves. The hair hanging from their necks was long and sweeping, as were their tails. Their legs, wide and muscular at the top, were narrow and slender at the bottom. Their feet had no toes, but were rounded like paws or hoofs.

And somewhere far, far away he saw 'dark clouds, angry clouds, and blood upon the land,' as if a Great Voice were speaking to him. The impression was so stark it echoed like words inside his head—

Dark clouds! Angry clouds!
...Blood upon the land!

And from the clouds the four great spirit-chiefs came leaping forward, led by a beast wearing a spotted robe, its hoofs drumming like thunder. From its eyes lightning flashed. And from the lightning came a rainbow of colors...and a magnificent wolf, galloping fast. It lifted him onto its back and raced along an invisible path where fires glowed and arrows flew as thick as a flock of birds. He saw his people being attacked by shadows, warriors from another tribe. The wolf spirit ran amongst them and he swiped at each shadow, scattering them with a simple wave of his hand. When they were gone, the wolf spirit leapt into the fire. The fire rose up. And there among the dark clouds, angry clouds, his vision ended, just as quiet and serene as when it started, the Great Voice whispering—

*"Tu-ra-hey."**

He stared into the emptiness of night long after it was over, reliving the experience again and again, until everything went suddenly black. And down he tumbled from the boulder. As if dead.

---

* "It is good."

Chapter 5

IT WAS SCARCELY LIGHT when vultures gathered on the crowns of the granite slabs, leering hungrily at the body sprawled in the grass below. They waited well past dawn and still there was no movement. Boldly, one of the vultures sprang from its perch, glided closer, landed with claws extended, and pecked at his shoulder. Opening an eye, Flying Fox felt something digging at his skin. He winced, turned, and slashed at the creature with a rock, but missed. The vulture cawed and took flight, as did the rest of the flock.

Dazed and sore all over, he settled back against a rock outcropping, nursing his wounds. His smashed hand—swollen and discolored from internal bleeding—now throbbed with pain. Blood trickled from his shoulder where he was bitten. His knees were stiff, out of joint, his back strained, and belly ached with hunger.

Although he suffered, he had reached a state of peace, knowing he had accomplished what he had set out to do.

In his mind the vision returned with remarkable clarity—the wolf spirits carrying him into battle, the shadows from an unknown tribe attacking his people, the arrows, the thunder, the lightning, the fires aglow—all of it told a story, foretelling the future, not only his, but the future of his people. And because he had seen the wolf-spirits, he believed they had revealed themselves for a reason. If nothing else, there was an unmistakable message, one darkly predicting war, yet he was convinced he would survive and would one day assure the survival of his people.

It became more evident when soon he learned he could walk, perhaps not with ease or youthful agility, but he preferred limping to crawling. Half crippled, he would never make it to the new village and without food and water he would die within a few days, but neither of these things seemed to worry him much. Food was everywhere, even during times of drought, and his body was limber enough to mend from any ache or bruise.

The distance between him and his tribe did not appear to present an insurmountable problem either. During their last night together, his father devised a system of markings that would not only reunite the two, but inform him of how the tribe was faring.

"The ground will be trodden bare where we walk," said Two Buffalo, "making a trail as big and wide as a herd of buffalo. Every night I will go to the tallest place near our camp and arrange some rocks. At each marker there will be a branch with a feather tied to it so you can see it from a distance. If all the rocks are light in color, it means we are doing well. One dark rock will tell of some small misfortune. A few dark rocks, trouble. Many dark rocks, death. If all are dark, many deaths, perhaps even war. No rocks, no marker...and you will know that I am dead."

The best place to rejoin the Trail of Rocks, Flying Fox reasoned, was where they separated, so off he limped into the land of the Long Grass, weaponless, without food and water, the vision of wolf-spirits a constant source of motivation. As time went on, the markers, each faithfully and prominently displayed, became a source of inspiration. Sometimes a surprise was tucked away among the rocks—a bag of corn meal, wampum, moccasins, and in keeping with late summer *When-Cherries-Turn-Black* (August) a buckskin coat to keep him warm when the weather cooled. But not once during the many moons which passed did he see a dark rock, so he assumed the fortunes of his people were good.

The food he ate was not. It was adequate at best, consisting mostly of wild turnips, onions, grouse, rabbit, roots, quail and duck eggs... nothing of what he craved—deer or buffalo meat. In time, he was able to regain most of his strength. He healed his wounds with herbs, bandaged his shoulder with leaves tied by strands of grass, and set his hand in a bush splint.

His recovery took almost twenty days and while the tracks of his people grew fresher each day, the trail seemed never-ending, his pursuit futile, even though he maintained a grueling pace of running from sunup to sundown.

Along the way, he saw tracks unlike any he had seen before. The animals ran in packs like buffalo, only the hoofs were larger, more oval-shaped, leaving a deep imprint, long and wide from one track to the next. It appeared the creatures were four-legged, equal in size and weight to a buffalo and roamed the land, grazing on grass.

On two occasions, both at night, he felt the ground shake and heard a stampeding of hoofs, thinking they were buffalo. They were not. They did not grunt or bellow like buffalo, instead neighed and whinnied, called to one another as if nervous or skittish. By the light of the day, he could tell the tracks had the same characteristics as those he had seen before, and for two nights he caught a glimpse of several pairs of eyes, each like coals from a fire, glowing in the dark, but the animals galloped off before he could get a closer look. Two things stood out in his mind, however: how fleet afoot they were and how long the strides appeared to be. Other animals may have been as fast—an antelope, a dog, or wolf perhaps—but nothing compared to the mysterious creatures as far as the amount of ground they covered when running.

Regrettably, the herd migrated south, *Where Summer Comes*, in search of fall grass and a warmer climate. His path, meanwhile, remained due west, toward the setting sun, never changing.

Late one morning, almost thirty moons into his journey, after two consecutive days of rain, high winds, and dark skies, the sun blossomed like a ripe, luscious flower. In the distance, rising ghostly, he noticed the outline of the Shiny Mountains. Peaks blanketed with snow soared to heights never before imagined. The valleys below loomed with a richness "feathered with trees," each slope radiant and distinctive in their majesty.

But their beauty was offset by the emergence of the first dark rock.

At the next marker more dark rocks appeared. By the third marker, he could tell by the scuffling of the tracks what had taken place. Up ahead, he saw buzzards circling a hill. On the other side of it, pooled in blood, were the sources of the terrible attraction. Many dead Pawnees! Their bodies were scattered throughout the high grass with arrows stuck in their bellies, their backs, and sides. Twenty-seven dead he counted, abandoned, with no grave scaffolds to honor them. Upon closer inspection, he saw they were not all Pawnees. Or warriors.

Bodies were lying everywhere, legs twisted, arms outstretched, swarms of insects buzzing…

It was a desecration to their spirit.

A boy he knew was among them. Running Elk was his name. Ten winters he lived—a tomahawk wedged deep in the middle of his spine.

A young girl was lying next to him. Willow Raven. Eight winters young. A beautiful child, a *pi-rau'*, who loved to dance and sing. Slain by an arrow. Never allowed to sing and dance again.

There were many others he recognized. Yellow Bird. Little Bear. Dull Knife. Red Hand. All slumped in pools of blood. Lumps of bone and muscle. Now just carrion. Soon to be eaten by Flesh Eaters—buzzard, vulture, and wandering prairie wolf—doing what they were born to do: scavenge as best they could.

A dusty wind blew. Dark clouds, angry clouds scudded across the blue sky. Beneath a grassy knoll, lifeless arms and legs were groping their way into the Spirit World, casualties of a bitter war.

From inside the battleground an old squaw wailed, mourning someone wrapped in a buffalo robe. Flying Fox recognized *Woman-by-the-River* by her streaks of graying hair. She was waving eagle feathers over the robe, rocking back and forth, squatting on her knees.

"We were attacked by Comanches," she moaned as Flying Fox walked up to her. "Your family is safe…with the others. Go to them. I will stay to bury my husband. Let the buzzards bury the Comanches!"

Flying Fox wanted to cry, but a warrior never cries.

He gathered up a bow, quiver, and handful of arrows bloodied from the battle. As he left, he glanced at the body of a dead Comanche, remembering the message implied in the vision: that he was chosen to repel all aggressors of his people.

As witness to the wolf-spirits, he vowed to rid the land of all Comanches, until all attempts failed, or he died trying.

He did not urge Woman-by-the-River to go with him, for she only wanted to bury her husband. After that, she would live out her usefulness, then die slowly—alone.

Chapter 6

HOW VASTLY DIFFERENT the mountains were from the plains. Rugged snow-capped peaks rose high into the sky, touching the clouds, as an expanse of firs, pines, and evergreens stretched across a succession of wide, deep valleys. The drought was not in evidence at all. The soil was moist and leaves, grass, and trees flourished in a climate much cooler than the prairie. Strange new tribes lived in and around the bordering lands—Ute, Crow, Shoshone. Dangerous animals, too.

Flying Fox had heard tales of the stealth of the mountain lion and savageness of the black bear. They had no equals to the flatlands to the east. Such creatures and the mysteries of the mountain tribes made him wary of this new country. Yet he was captivated in ways he had never experienced. The mountains were more confining, unlike the openness of the grasslands. And sounds echoed without dying in the wind.

He walked for two days through the foothills following the trail of the Pawnee migration and saw countless animal tracks and more kinds of species than there were cows, bulls, and calves in an entire herd of buffalo. There were sheep, elk, deer, grizzly. Mountain lion, beaver, moose. Every conceivable type of rodent. An endless variety of birds. Gray squirrels, black squirrels, brown squirrels. Rabbits by the score. Foxes, weasels, skunks, otters, wolves, coyotes. But no buffalo. No *taraha*. That was the one big disappointment. No massive, plodding beast, running in herds.

In the mountains water abounded everywhere, winding through valleys and dense forests, pouring over cliffs, filling up basins with clean, cool lakes. Stream after stream he crossed, wading through currents fast and slow, barely above freezing. It was during the fording of a steep, fast-moving rapids that his life was about to change, forever. He encountered two animals, one of which was so unusual he had no idea what to make of it. The other...

He was wading hip-deep in water when he spotted a grizzly foraging for food in a thicket of pines. Quietly, stepping from rock to rock through the rushing water, Flying Fox reached the far bank. Crouching among the bushes, he placed an arrow in his bow. The bear immediately sensed something. It lifted its head, snorted at the air, and picked up his scent. Before it could react, it was distracted by a cry deep in the forest. Echoing through the trees came a peal of laughter. Ahead, through a maze of pines, hoof beats were rapidly approaching. Both the grizzly and the young Pawnee were prepared to attack, or defend themselves if necessary. Flying Fox had his bowstring pulled, the arrow ready. His line of sight wavered back and forth from the bear to a trail winding through a forest.

Down the slope of the mountain, ambling twice as fast as any buffalo, came a beast the likes of which he had never seen, ridden by a warrior from an unknown tribe.

How queer this beast was! Spotted brown and white. Long, lean muscular legs and stout body. A mane of hair flowing from its neck. Tail swishing gently behind. Could it be a giant, short-haired wolf?

Flying Fox was stunned. Another part of his vision quest had come true. The wolf-spirit was no longer just a dream!

He watched in awe as the warrior yanked on a rope tied around the animal's neck. Rider and beast stopped. The rider got down and knelt by the water's edge while the wolf bent its head to take a drink.

From the pines to their right, the sound of heavy paws thumped through the brush. Frothing at the mouth, the hulking form lumbered towards them, snapping twigs and branches underfoot while thrusting all of its massive weight in the effort. In doing so, it left no doubt of its intention. Narrow-set eyes were fixed on its prey, massive muscles rippling, driven mad by an insatiable appetite, its entire being in a ravenous state of fury. It would stop at nothing to get to its kill.

Uncertain what to do, Flying Fox feared for their lives, as well as his own. Disregarding all thought of himself, he took aim upon the bear and released an arrow, striking the animal in the upper foreleg. Stunned, the raging bear snarled, limped awkwardly for a moment, but kept charging, riled all the more. Aroused by the scent of meat, instead of turning and retreating, it increased its abandon. It labored in spite of the arrow lodged deep in the bone where spurts of blood were gushing, a wound so deep, any lesser animal would have given up and retreated. Not this one. This one was incredibly strong and vicious, driven by a craving for meat.

The giant wolf, aware of the threat, suddenly panicked. It whinnied and drew back, terrified, as the rider tried to leap onto its back. The wolf reared up and the rider fell to the ground, holding a rope strapped to the animal's neck.

Shocked by the strength of the charging beast, Flying Fox reacted quickly. He shot another arrow, then a third, each hitting the mark, one below the breast, the other next to it. The bear, in deep spasms of pain, plodded a few steps and stopped, trying to shake the arrows off. One leg buckled, then a second. It rolled over, growling, coughing up blood. A fourth arrow struck, this time puncturing the neck. The creature slumped on its side, legs twitching, groaning, expending its final breath.

All at once, three more riders of wolves converged on the path. They saw Flying Fox holding a bow, the first rider struggling with his mount, and must have thought the first rider was in danger, not out of it, for they quickly surrounded the Pawnee and raised their tomahawks to strike.

"No!"

A cry averted the riders and they lowered their tomahawks. The first warrior, the one whose life had been saved, laughed when he saw the look of surprise on Flying Fox's face.

"Good for me you hunt better than the bear," he said, motioning to the body lying among the pines. When the others saw the bear, they realized their mistake. They simply nodded and smiled.

Given the excitable nature of the kill, they wasted no time in acquainting themselves with each other and the bear. What a massive brute it was, measuring three heads taller than the tallest man there and weighing at least three times that of the heaviest man. Its paw, when held against a hand, wrapped around the fist completely, with the length of its claws to spare. Along the back and across the bear's face, from eye to muzzle, and at the bottom of its neck, were several deep scars, long purplish lines of serrated skin, now totally healed, covered by thick, raggedy patches of hair where battles against other bears and other predators had been won and lost.

Flying Fox learned the warriors were from a small tribe of Apaches called the *Paducahs*, a peaceful band of nomads who had migrated from the southern plains because of a long and continuous drought. What interested Flying Fox the most, however, aside from their affable nature, was the manner in which Paducahs dressed. Each wore a buckskin shirt. Strips of leather hanging from their sleeves were worn as ornamentation. From their necks to their feet, they were covered in leather, fine intricate skins cut from buffalo and deer, each piece decorated with painted symbols, designs, appliqué, ribbons, beaded aprons across the front of their leggings, deer roaches, sashes, belts, necklaces made of either porcupine quill, bear claw, or the claw of a panther. Around their elbows they wore beaded arm bands, around their knees leg bands, all topped by roaches, bonnets fashioned from quill, eagle and hawk feathers.

The difference in their garments was only slight. To a man they were clothed lavishly, having costumes more in keeping with ceremony than use every day.

But it wasn't the extravagant clothing or the bear that eventually won Flying Fox's attention. It was something else. The lead warrior noticed the peculiar way Flying Fox kept looking at the creatures they rode. "Why do you look at our horses like that?" he asked.

"Horses?" Flying Fox replied. "I know of no horses. I once had a vision where beasts came to me as wolf-spirits. One of them carried me on its back. Is the horse some kind of wolf?"

"I do not doubt your vision, but a wolf is smaller and wild," said the Paducah. "I do not think it is a wolf."

"To me it is a giant wolf, tame as a dog," said Flying Fox. He thought for a moment and asked, "Would you trade it for something? For this bear perhaps?"

"I owe you my life," said the Paducah. "Anything of mine is yours."

"Good. I will call it *Giant Wolf*."

The Paducahs all smiled.

Unable to restrain himself, Flying Fox jumped on the animal's back, hoping to ride away. How foolish he was. Giant Wolf whinnied, spun, and started forward with an unexpected lurch, flinging its new rider to the ground.

The Paducahs all burst into laughter. They doubled over, grinning and slapping at each other, as if it were the silliest thing they had ever seen.

By no means discouraged, but carefully this time, Flying Fox tried to mount the animal once more. He jumped on its back, and again Giant Wolf spun, bucked, burst into a run, and once more inexperience overcame desire, and rider, with elbows and knees flailing, was tossed unceremoniously to the ground.

The Paducahs hooted and howled with uncontrollable glee as they helped him to his feet. Unhurt, except for his pride, Flying Fox brushed himself off and laughed along with the rest of them. They soon became fast friends and the Paducahs offered to teach him the techniques of riding.

They taught him how to hold the rope, how to lead left and right for the desired direction. They showed him how to curl his legs around the sides to remain seated, then how to kick and run and make the animal stop. They taught him the subtler persuasions as well—how to hold the horse to a trot, when to let it walk, how to snap the rope and kick together to make it jump, what to say and how to say it when giving a command. In time, he learned the basic fundamentals: how to treat the creature, what to feed it, how it slept, how to care for it, how to groom it, and in general everything he needed to know. The lessons took the better part of two days, until the new rider gained enough confidence to act on his own.

Below a ridge, they made a campfire and settled in for a good night's sleep, sharing a meal of roasted bear meat. Tough though it was, one of the Paducahs remarked that nothing tasted better, especially when it could have been the bear who was doing the eating, not the other way around.

By the end of the second day, Flying Fox had taken to the horse as well as anyone could under the circumstances. To his credit, he became very adept at riding and caring for the animal, especially for someone so raw and fresh to the skills of horsemanship. He sat proud and high, thrilled by Giant Wolf's speed. He could feel the wind when there was no wind. He could ride through a stream and not get wet, venture through a mountain range that would take days to walk. As he rode, there was a special excitement about having another living thing do as you want, and do it with grace, such willingness, and yes, so fast. He was like a hawk, flying in a wind of passion, gliding effortlessly without wings. And to feel the power trampling beneath, the long, loping legs carrying him where sights sped dizzily by—it was an absolute wonder. Joy! He had never felt anything like it, not even in a dream or vision.

"You have been very good to me," he said to his teachers at last.

"But now I must go. The Paducahs are a great people to give such a gift as this. Giant Wolf and I will come visit you some day. Until then, grow strong from the bear meat, my friends."

The Paducahs waved farewell.

Their leader yelled, "We will see each other again, Pawnee! *Hoy-ahhh!*"

*   *   *

Despite all the lessons, mishaps, and progress he had made, riding a horse was not easy as he expected. Nor was Giant Wolf entirely pleased with having a stranger sitting on its back. Generally, it obeyed his commands, but there were times when it was headstrong, when it felt free to run at its own pace, not one dictated by somebody else. It often acted skittish, either because it was unfamiliar with the territory or the direction it was headed, or a situation presented itself—a pack of wolves crossing a ravine, a mountain lion prowling the bushes—which demanded caution and no amount of discipline or persuasion could change its mind. Several times it stopped dead in its tracks and, with its right front hoof, pawed at the ground, a sure sign danger was lurking nearby.

Fortunately, both lion and wolf were cautious of the horse. And of the rider.

Overall, Flying Fox was happy with the way the horse responded, how he adjusted to it, and it to him. It was smart, obedient, agile, strong, and extraordinarily fast. It seemed the *Nabu'rac* had created a four-legged animal perfectly suited for speed, one whose heart and desire were equal to the rapid pace it set. As the day wore on, he could tell when it was tiring, when it was hungry, when it was thirsty, or by the way it held its tail, the type of mood it was in. Through observation, he became more and more acquainted with it and it to him and the two developed a relationship based on mutual trust. On his part, Flying Fox assumed nothing and was always worried about the animal running away.

What surprised him the most about riding, however, was not related to the horse, but to himself. His flexibility was always being tested. A sudden lunge, dodging right, dodging left, could easily throw him off balance. Twice he fell. The first time he thought he had broken a rib. The second fall, a shoulder. Fortunately, neither time did it turn out to be the case.

The other thing that was surprising was endurance. Stamina. Sitting on a powerful animal whose back was as hard as wood, while bouncing up and down, made for a very uncomfortable experience. His legs cramped. His backside grew sore. His arms, shoulders, and spine all suffered as well. And when he dismounted after a full day of riding, his legs felt as if they had been disjointed at the knees, bent outward like a bowstring. He limped around, feeling the effects on every bone, every muscle, from his hips to his feet, from his backbone to his neck.

It was all a part of a process of learning how to ride, and from the first moment he sat upon the animal until now—through the heavy falls, the failed responses, his ineptness, the strong-headedness of the animal—it was wondrous and thrilling. As if it were a dream.

There were steps he had to take, sacrifices he had to make, both of which he was quite willing to do. And to do it in the Land of the Shiny Mountains with a creature he had seen in a vision…it was more re-markable than anything he could possibly imagine. And so he rode—awestruck, yet vigilant—through most of the remaining day.

From a mountain pass, he saw spectacular colors, bands of blue, green, red, and gold, arching over a valley basking in sunshine. The rainbow was the result of a recent rain shower. Below stretched a placid lake, stilled by the absence of wind. On one side of the lake was a forest of evergreens; on the other, the charred remains of a forest fire. From the ashes rose saplings and ferns. Above ground stood the blackened trunks of firs and pines and charred stubs that were once branches.

To the north and west, mountain ranges were crammed with a profusion of trees, ascending to peaks of rock covered in snow.

The air was fresh and clear and exhilarating. He almost felt like he could see forever. His father once said that if you watched long enough and your eyes were good, you would always see a sign of the *Nabu'rac* at work, a life and death struggle among the brotherhood of animals. Whether a snake or field mouse, fox or rabbit, carnivore against carnivore, bear against wolf—it was how animals existed. Some lived, some died. It was how things were—the way of the *Nabu'rac*.

High atop the slopes, far away from coyotes and wolves, sheep with brownish-gray coats, some with horns curling at the sides of their heads, were standing sure-footed in places where one misstep would end in tragedy, a fall from a precipitous height. One brave creature, a rugged old ram with a large set of horns, had thrown all caution to the wind and was slurping water from a river when it raised up and sensed something wrong.

The Pawnees call it *na-hond-zad*: "Fearing time." "Time of fear." And for good reason.

Crouched nearby, a pack of wolves made its way along the edge of the bank and suddenly took off in pursuit. Familiar as the sheep was with the territory and makeup of the terrain, it proved its superiority by climbing a steep slope comprised of boulders, large outcroppings, and crags of stone, leaving the wolves frustrated at the base of the rocky slope.

Another drama, meanwhile, was unfolding elsewhere.

A great bald eagle screeched as it circled the valley. It glided over a forest, across the lake, swooped down, and came away with a fish clutched in its talons, the tail of which was still flapping. Back to the rim of the summit the eagle soared, ready to feast on the delicacy or feed it to the young chicks nesting there.

Two Buffalo once said, when traveling through an unfamiliar land, a man stood a better chance of remembering it if he gave it a name. So Flying Fox gave each landmark, each body of water a name as he crossed it. First, he crossed Big Bear Creek, then Rainbow Lake, between Fire and Eagle Mountains, and now stood atop a mountain pass, overlooking the Valley of the Bighorn River. Below, the Bighorn wound its way to an even larger chain of mountains, stretching as far as the eye could see.

Somewhere between Big Bear Creek, Rainbow Lake, and Fire Mountain, he picked up the trail of his people. It was just before dusk and the sun was shining. As he stopped to study the tracks, he began to detect the presence of smoke. He could see no fires, but the peaks ahead were divided by a crescent-shaped gorge suitable for a number of camps—hidden among the trees perhaps, secreted in the valley somewhere, but promising enough to give him hope. The problem was, the ridge wasn't tall enough to see above the treetops. Still, his instincts told him he was getting close—

Very, very close.

Down into the valley he rode, thinking of Two Buffalo and Musk Raven, waiting by the freshly-made lodges, smiling upon his return. The trees thinned into clearings at the mouth of a river while the tracks in the soggy soil grew sharper and fresher. Through an opening in the trees he saw patches of gray swirling up into the sky.

Suddenly, the heart of man and hoofs of beast beat swiftly, hurried on by the traces of smoke.

These were Pawnee campfires!

He soon learned, however, there would be no celebration. Dogs were barking and drums were pounding, alerting the camp of plunder as Pawnee warriors called out to engage in battle.

Giant Wolf leapt over some bushes and a gulley, then burst through the last barrier—a thicket of long branched trees—between them and the encampment. A flurry of violence erupted as a Comanche war party attacked a party of Pawnees pitched near a stand of pines. Arrows flew back and forth from one side to the other amid the blare of war cries.

Flying Fox rode abreast the most perilous point, causing both sides to stop and stare in shocked amazement. He seized a spear, reared up on his mount, and—with a frantic, reckless shout—kicked Giant Wolf into a gallop, heading straight for the enemy. He closed upon them and poked the blunt end of the spear at one…two…three Comanches!

They fled, escaping into the trees, as he continued to *count coup*.* Four…five…six Comanches! They were driven up the slope, scattering like deer from a panther.

---

* an attack whereby an enemy is touched only

Seven...eight...nine...

The Pawnees cheered.

* * *

That night a highly respected warrior was honored during a feast in the Pawnees' new village. As everyone stood around the campfires, the chief remarked that only Two Buffalo's son could ride on the back of a wolf and count Comanche coup.

The chief gave him a name. He called him *Wolf Rider*.

"Wolf Rider! Wolf Rider!" they shouted.

Young maidens gazed at a tall pose set against the firelight. Wolf-Rider sat upon Giant Wolf and told the story of his vision quest. The people listened and imagined the wolf spirits rising from the Stone Lodges to carry a young brave on his ride with destiny.

BOOK THREE: WOLF RIDER
Shadowless Man

Chapter 7

Pawnee Death Song:
>"Listen, my brother! That is not the wind you hear.
>But the wail of a spirit in mourning as it
>echoes through the trees."

SECLUDED IN A SMALL CLEARING, the six burial platforms served as a reminder of battle. Each body was wrapped in a buffalo hide with the head of the animal intact, resting upon the skull of the deceased. Shields, weapons, and other personal items—such as a sash, bracelet, or headdress—were placed on the scaffolds to identify the victim by name, clan, and stature.

In a pitched camp nearby, men were cutting down trees, chopping logs, building frames for tepees, making the land suitable as a temporary home. Scattered throughout the valley, sentries stood guard, armed with bows and arrows, watching the surrounding mountains for signals from scouts, warning of a possible attack by Comanche war parties. In their haste to settle in before nightfall, no one was spared an idle moment.

Boy, girl, the young and the old, everyone was busy, collecting branches, scraps of wood, or assisting in the making of the tepees. Perhaps the busiest of all were the squaws who hurried about, building campfires, preparing feasts while tribal leaders discussed a grave matter in council.

Summoned as its newest member, Wolf Rider entered the smoke-filled lodge to find everyone seated and the discussion underway. Presiding over the meeting were the chief and war chief who listened as a pipe was passed around the circle of warriors. After each man smoked, he would speak.

The lodge sounded with dark voices. War! Now! Against the Comanches! To avenge the dead and those injured in battle, everyone boasted of the fierceness with which they would fight. Threats and promises of victory rang out, accompanied by the beating of a single drum.

When the pipe was handed to Wolf Rider, the drum stopped and war chief said, "There is one who has not spoken yet. What does the man who counted coupe and is admired by all the young women say?"

Wolf Rider smoked, then slowly and with deliberation replied, "My heart grows sad by the loss of our people. Our brothers fought bravely I am told." He was interrupted by a burst of chatter—praise in support of the fallen warriors. He waited for the response to die down, carefully choosing his words. "Before we attack the Comanches, we should make ourselves stronger, not weaker."

Rattles shook and men whispered. Not to attack? The chief and war chief talked briefly, then turned, and asked for an explanation.

With fire in his voice, Wolf Rider said, "If each of us owned a giant wolf, we would be strong. In war no one could defeat us. We could ride in one morning what would take days to walk. No buffalo could outrun us. We could hunt in distant lands and bring home meat, enough to feed *all* of our families. This we could do in a day or two without risk to our lives. There would be no hunger, no place where we could not go. We would be envied by our friends. Feared by our enemies. So I ask you this—is it riches you want? Peace? Food for our hungry children? Or a war without giant wolves. A war we may lose if we attack now?"

Reaction was swift, loud, and divided—some in support, some in opposition. Men got to their feet and started arguing. So passionate were their beliefs, no one was willing to let anyone else speak.

The war chief raised his hand for quiet, waited, then said to Wolf Rider, "You are against war?"

"I am not against war. But among the Paducahs I have a friend who owns many giant wolves. Maybe he would make a trade for something."

A pipe was handed to the war chief. He took a puff and asked, "And what would you use for this trade?"

"Buffalo skins. Bows, arrows. Knives. Anything we are willing to give. But gifts alone are not enough."

Again, there were whispers, followed by a loud, tremulous shaking of rattles.

And again the war chief motioned for silence. "Not enough? What more can we do?"

"First, we must first show that we go in peace…"

Speaking with words wise beyond his age, Wolf Rider outlined a simple but clever plan. The Council listened and was so impressed, warriors and priests shook their rattles and talked excitedly, nodding their heads in approval as sentiment quickly swung in his favor.

All this time the chief and war chief consulted at length. Finally, a decision was reached. War would be postponed until a trade had been made with the Paducahs.

Later that evening, there was a big feast in the middle of the campgrounds, also dancing and talk of the trade. Drums pounded and people danced while holy men and medicine healers, the *hataali*, prayed to the east where peace and light come; then to the south, which offers warmth; then to the west, which brings rain; and finally, to the north, with its cold and lashing winds that build strength and endurance.

In the morning, Wolf Rider prepared for the journey by grooming himself with the utmost of care. He did so by bathing in the cold waters of a stream, then selected each article of clothing as if he were attending a Buffalo Dance as a member of the *Hedushka.** As was customary of the *pariki*, Horn of the Bull, he stiffened his scalp with grease. To one lock of hair, he tied a roach of deer's tail. To another, a string of feathers. He put on his finest leggings and most colorful shirt, both made of softened deer hide. To top it off, he hung buckskin badge across his chest which shone with the beaded symbol of the sun.

When he emerged from his skin-covered lodge, he caught the eye of many admiring girls, especially Paw Dancer and Wallow Woman, his handsome unwed cousins who, according to rumor, were eager to marry. The sisters wore garlands in their hair, beautifully embroidered

---

* ceremonial society

dresses decorated with quills, beads, and sashes made for special oc-casions.

A Crier went throughout the camp, yelling, "Come! Wolf Rider is leaving to make a trade with the Paducahs. Hurry! Bring your knives, your tomahawks, your bracelets, everything you can give! Show him how generous the *Wolf Pa'ni* can be."

And, promptly, people came. They stood and watched as Wolf Rider attached a *travois*, a set of long wooden poles, to Giant Wolf's back, so the poles could be dragged along and used for hauling. Then, one by one, gifts were laid at his feet. Musk Raven presented a blanket, which she had woven, Two Buffalo a bow and quiver of arrows, while others donated buffalo hides, pelts, knives, pendants, and jewelry.

Of the gifts, there was one by an old man—a medicine pipe made of fruitwood—of great significance. When smoked, it had a fruity, nut-ty, apple-cherry taste to it. The detail, when compared to others, was unsurpassed. A portion was painted with orange, green, yellow, red, and blue stripes. Plumes of colorful birds hung from its clay-fired bowl and long wooden stem, combining for not only function and purpose, but the very thing it was supposed to inspire. Handcrafted with care and precision, it epitomized such rarity of skill it seemed to have some medicinal qualities as well. To see it was to cherish it and to cherish it was to realize that when smoked, peace was practically impossible to resist, given the effect it had.

Wolf Rider was indeed inspired by the gift, more so when the giv-er said, "Let the sacred hoop be unbroken. Walk quietly. And share the pipe in peace."

All around him, warriors and chiefs who attended the informal gathering offered words of encouragement.

Of the many concerns they had, there was one that outweighed all the others. The chief asked Wolf Rider who he had chosen to go with him and Wolf Rider responded by pointing at his two cousins and the maker of the pipe.

"What?" cried the chief. "An old man? And two young squaws?"

"My cousins are hungry for adventure," Wolf Rider explained. "And Lone Elk, old as he is, is still a great hunter."

The chief was not pleased at all. He motioned to the crowd and four men stepped forward. Two were brothers, armed and ready for battle—Black Eagle and Deer Slayer—who wore streaks of paint on their faces. The third, whose name was Ice Bear, was a tracker of great skill, fearless, without peer when it came to following a trail. The forth was an imposing figure of a man clad in buckskin. He had stooped shoulders, a purplish scar running along the left side of his neck. In his hand was a bow; across his back, a quiver of arrows; tucked in his waistband, a tomahawk, spiked club, and sheath with a long knife stuck inside it. His name was War Hawk, and of all the warriors he was the fiercest. In war, it was said he could bash a head from a body with a single stroke of a of a war club, and when provoked, could intimidate the most courageous and ablest of fighters.

"These are the men who will go with you," the chief announced. "I have chosen each myself." To guarantee them safe passage, he removed a bear-claw necklace and hung it around War Hawk's neck.

"Be strong, my friend. Go in peace." Then to the crowd he said, "*Wolf Pa'ni*, their success comes from you, from the heart, from the spirit. And though we do not know where the trail will lead, you can safely guide them through it. Let us pray their return is swift, bearing gifts, not just one, but many…so that all of us have horses. Ride the Giant Wolf! *Loo-ah*! Go! Your chief has spoken."

Once everything was packed, a priest, a maker of *ti-war' uks-ti*,* sprinkled dust over the travois in the hopes of bringing them prosperity. Wallow Woman and Paw Dancer climbed on the horse's back while Lone Elk, Ice Bear, War Hawk, Wolf Rider, and two brothers, Black Eagle and Deer Slayer, walked behind. Under the watchful eye of the chief, they departed with the rest of the tribe looking on.

For half a day they journeyed, passing between Fire and Eagle Mountains, around Rainbow Lake, on their way to Big Bear Creek. The air was warm and fresh and filled with sunshine. Aspen, fir, and pine, and colors of a changing season accompanied them throughout their travels in the High Country. Often the howls of wolves and roars of mountain panthers echoed through the forest. Now and again, white-tailed deer, fearing for their lives, escaped soundlessly into the trees, only to be attacked and killed later in a thrashing melee of gore and blood.

---

* magic

It was now the *Moon of the Black Calf* (August) and by late after-noon, thanks to Ice Bear, they finally found the place where Wolf Rider had killed the bear. Beside a stream, they saw footprints and marks in the soil made by the poles of a travois, so they followed the tracks, trying to make as little noise as possible. At the base of the mountains they crossed another stream and entered a forest separating the moun-tains from the hills to the northeast.

The silence and stillness of the forest seemed out of character for a place teeming with birds and wild creatures. A quiet forest meant a guarded forest, a forbidden forest, a forest where small creatures hid from big creatures and big creatures from the most dangerous creatures of all: People. The path was narrow, often overgrown with underbrush, with plants that itched when you touched them, plants with thorns that scratched and clawed and drew blood if you didn't watch where you were going. And when the trees and bushes were too thick to pass, they found a shallow stream to cross. Advancement was slow and te-dious, but they learned to make their way as best they could, moving quietly in single file. One or two of the warriors were always scouting ahead, with weapons drawn, eyes constantly probing the thickets for deer or possible ambush.

There were moments, however, when they were taken by sur-prise. A rotted tree fell once, collapsing from decay, and toppled with a loud crash. A nest of quail went flying across the trail, screeching, as the party approached. With the practiced eye of a hunter and reflexes amazingly quick, Lone Elk shot a quail in mid-flight, the arrow ripping through its breast.

The day, otherwise, went without incident. It was a day marked by hunger, uncertainty, and a growing apprehension on the part of the sisters.

Through water, mud, and endless thicket they trudged, negotiat-ing rocks, steep hills, and trails that hindered with nagging persistence. At one point, tired and worried they had gotten lost, Wallow Woman asked how close they were to the Paducah village. Wolf Rider answered by shrugging his shoulders and shaking his head.

During one of their infrequent stops, she said, "I hear strange peo-ple live in the mountains. *Ute. Moache. Copote.* People who hide under trees and never see daylight. My mother told me of a tribe called the

Hopi who live in stone lodges, eat the meat of snakes, and speak a language I have never heard before. I wonder if the Paducahs have strange ways and strange words."

"Do not worry," said Wolf Rider. "The Paducahs do not eat the meat of snakes. If you worry too much, maybe you should go home."

But Wallow Woman and her sister had no desire to go home. Their desire, he suspected, had nothing to do with adventure and everything to do with the dresses they wore.

That evening, under a ledge of sheltering rock they made camp, eating roasted quail and rabbit while lying on beds of moss and fur.

With darkness came a brisk autumn chill and the howling of wolves. Wallow Woman and Paw Dancer curled up in blankets and slept peacefully while War Hawk stayed up all night keeping the campfire burning. Before sunup, he told Wolf Rider he and Black Eagle and Deer Slayer were going to scout ahead.

"The tracks lead through those trees," he whispered, pointing at a cluster of pines. "Do not wait for us. We will return when we know it is safe." And off they went, without a sound, disappearing like shadows into the night.

At dawn, Wolf Rider followed the Trail of the Slain Bear, wandering through deep, dark forests—with Lone Elk and Ice Bear on foot and Wallow Woman and Paw Dancer sitting on Giant Wolf. At a small creek they stopped to take a drink. It was here that Wolf Rider heard the sound of a twig snapping. He slowly walked over to a tree, using it to protect his back, and signaled to his cousins and Lone Elk and Ice bear to do the same. Suddenly, an arrow struck a tree, sending everyone diving into the underbrush. A second arrow whistled overhead, knocking leaves from branches, coming harmlessly to rest in a thicket beyond.

On the far side of the creek, laughter erupted. Moments later, a brave from an unknown tribe walked into the clearing, grinning, holding a feathered bow in one hand, his belly with the other.

"The Pawnee sleeps as he walks," he joked. "Maybe he is not man enough to have two brides."

Wolf Rider answered, not with words, but by taking playful aim. He shot an arrow, striking the tree between the brave's legs. The brave in turn dropped his jaw, gaping at the quivering arrow stuck between his knees. This time it was Wolf Rider who laughed—that is, until he felt the point of a knife digging into his spine.

"If you run," a man warned, "I will cut out your heart and feed it to the wolves."

*   *   *

The Pawnees caused quite a stir in the alien camp, tied up and dressed as they were. A pack of dogs came running, barking wildly, snapping at their feet, followed by dirty-faced children, rowdy and bare-footed, who taunted and counted coup with their grubby, little hands.

"*He-ya! He-ya!* " they screamed.

All throughout the camp, people dropped what they were doing and stood around, gawking and staring, to see what the commotion was about. Led by riders on horseback, the captives were taken to a tepee where, beside it, hung a bear hide on a drying rack. There, bound and lashed together, the captives were shoved to the ground.

People swarmed around them, shouting, jeering, poking them with the blunt end of spears. All at once a hand reached out, clutching a knife, and started cutting the bindings loose.

"We have strange ways of meeting, Pawnee," a man shouted.

The crowd stood back and suddenly grew quiet.

Wolf Rider recognized the face of the warrior he once saved.

"It is good to see my brother of the bear."

"And it is good to see the gifted hunter," replied the Paducah.

Addressing his fellow tribesmen, he said, "These are my friends. Go! Bother them no more!"

One by one, the crowd began to disperse.

"I do not know your name," remarked the Paducah. "I am *Man Who Hunts the Moon.*"

Wolf Rider introduced himself, his cousins, and in passing, Ice Bear and Lone Elk.

Man Who Hunts the Moon smiled at the two young women, then gestured to the tepee behind him. "Bring your wives. The old man and the other one, too. Your horse and skins will be taken care of."

Before entering the tepee, Wolf Rider looked around at the village and saw many horses. Black ones, brown ones, chestnuts, sorrels.

Many dogs, too, and row after row of beautiful skin lodges. On their sides were painted buffalo, elk, deer, horses, the sun and the moon. But nowhere did he see a sign of War Hawk or the two missing braves, Black Eagle and Deer Slayer.

After a quick explanation, Wolf Rider asked if anyone had seen a Pawnee with a scar running along his neck or two brothers with paint on their faces.

The Paducah replied that he had not seen a stranger for days and gave his assurances a party of scouts would be sent to look for them.

"Wherever they are, we will find them. Come! I have food inside."

Soon the sisters, Lone Elk, and Ice Bear were squatting in one corner of the tepee while Wolf Rider sat opposite Man Who Hunts the Moon. The two exchanged pleasantries, after which they ate, drank, smoked, and joked about their first encounter. Wolf Rider made no mention of the trade yet, but did remark tactfully the sisters weren't his wives, but his cousins.

This interested Man Who Hunts the Moon. He began to flirt with both and they reacted by blushing and giggling as young women often do.

He is pleased with them, Wolf Rider thought.

Indeed, the Paducah's pleasure was so great, after a while he ignored Wolf Rider altogether and went and sat between the fair sisters where his charms could be applied more closely. They talked for the longest time and never once did a smile leave the Paducah's face. His playful hands fluttered from woman to woman like butterflies over ripe flowers, dancing from nectar to nectar.

To endear him even more, Wolf Rider said, "Wallow Woman is not only beautiful, she is gifted with both gentle and strong hands. Her touch is warm and soft. And she can weave, cook, and sew. Best of all, she sing songs which can arouse even a spirit. And Paw Dancer, as you can see, is as lovely as her sister. She can heal a wound whether it is in the heart or of the flesh. And as her name will prove, she can dance as well.

"Sing Wallow Woman! Dance Paw Dancer! Show Man Who Hunts the Moon!"

The Paducah's eyes popped wide with amusement as he watched and listened to the talents of the Pawnee sisters. Wallow Woman's voice trilled and swooned while Paw Dancer moved in graceful rhythm. No sooner had the performance started when a man poked his head inside the tepee. A smile broadened on his face, then drew down in irritation as he was bumped from behind. A second man soon appeared, then a third, a fourth, each of them grinning. In spite of his host's desire for privacy, Wolf Rider went to the entrance and pulled the flap open. As he did, a score of men came stumbling in. No invitation needed. They all piled around to gape and stare while Wallow Woman joined her sister in dance and Paw Dancer her sister in song, and together they shook and quivered and trilled and raised the blood to a boil.

All the while Wolf Rider slapped his thighs like drums and grinned along with the rest of them.

Chapter 8

"There is no good without evil,
no health without sickness,
no riches without poverty,
and no abundance without hunger."

– Black Elk
from *Black Elk Speaks*

IT WAS HARD TO LEAVE such a happy, warm-hearted people. But Wolf Rider was ready to return home. Paw Dancer married Man Who Hunts the Moon and four men courted Wallow Woman so fiercely the prospective husbands fought every day until the wedding. Eventually, she was won by a young suitor named Calf Robe. In exchange for the gifts he gave, and, as part of the dowries offered by the grooms, Wolf Rider received six giant wolves, a sacred bundle containing hawk feathers, the claw of a grizzly, and a black stone intended to bring good fortune.

Not everything went so smoothly, however. There were jealousies, petty differences, even a rift about how a highly prized bearskin was obtained. Stories varied. Feelings were hurt and soothed again by a game of sorts. At stake was the highly prized bearskin, the one that introduced Wolf Rider to the Paducahs in the first place. To acquire it, the daring young Pawnee had to employ some shrewdness. Using his father's gift of bow and arrow and Lone Elk's ability to hit a target, he arranged a match between the Paducah's best bowman and the old man. The contest brought whoops and hollers and a huge surprise. Lone Elk out-dueled the younger Paducah by hitting a mark on a tree at sixty paces, then bettered him again by walking ten paces farther and striking the target with ease. As a result, two more horses were won and added to the cause.

Eight in all!

The marriages took place in three days, the festivities in four. Twice Wolf Rider was made a '*blood brother*' of the respective grooms and he ceaselessly ate, danced, sang, and told or was told an endless number of stories.

And once again, on festive occasions and those more serious, no one proved more invaluable than Lone Elk. In gratitude of his pipe, a deep alliance was made and bonds were formed between families and friends and tribes as well, and by use of sign language, he was able to instill his knowledge of Pawnee culture by helping build an earth lodge in the center of camp. As a type of entertainment during a feast one night, he threw kernels of dried corn into a fire and watched everyone jump when the kernels started popping.

Soon word spread of the stranger who did the '*hand talk*' and carried '*magic popping seeds*.' Affectionately, they called him *Old Man of the Forest* because his skin was wrinkled—like the bark of a tree. Wherever he went, day or night, children followed, skipping playfully after him, wondering what surprises were in store for them next. He showed them games, how to shoot arrows, how to plant corn for the coming spring *When-Tree-Buds-Turn-to-Leaves*, and enriched their lives in so many ways both the children and their parents wanted him to stay.

He often regaled his listeners with stories, fables passed down from generation to generation, which were always amusing, especially the tale of the Old Trickster, Coyote.

One evening, Lone Elk told a group of Paducahs, "Grandson was always asking questions of his grandfather. And this is what grandson asked—

> "*Grandfather, who was the first to make fire?*"
> "*The first to make fire, Grandson, were the Firefly People.*"
> "*And the rain? Could you tell me where it came from?*"
> "*Yes, Little One. I will tell you. It came from the Cloud People.*"
> "*And the Sun, Big Water (ocean), and the Wind? How did*
>   *they come to be?*"

"Those are big questions, Grandson. I am tired. But if you must know, I will tell you.

"There was once a thief named Coyote. No one was more clever than he. One day he stole light from the Firefly People and gave it to Sky Father. The next day he stole water from the Cloud People and gave it to Earth Mother. The third day, he stole a breath from a witch while she was sleeping, and he gave it to Sky Father. And that is how the Sun, Big Water, and Wind came to be."

The children loved hearing stories about the Old Trickster, Coyote. They asked Lone Elk to repeat the one about the *Sun, Big Water, and Wind* many times before going to bed. By the fourth day, Lone Elk—or Old Man of the Forest—because of his skills and knack for story telling, was adopted into the Paducah tribe.

So, too, did Ice Bear ingratiate himself to the Paducahs. He did it by falling in love with a maiden named Corn Woman, a mere child to some, but she had no family. Everybody felt sorry for her. Not Ice Bear. He was stricken by her smile as if struck by a bolt of lightning. He fell victim to a dizziness of sorts, fainting spells. His knees wobbled and eyes rolled up in his head, swooning, whenever he was around Corn Woman. Three days later they were married and Ice Bear became a Paducah forever.

All of this, of course, was tempered by the fact War Hawk and the two Pawnee brothers, Black Eagle and Deer Slayer, were never found. Paducah scouts searched everywhere—on horseback, on foot, in the mountains, through hills, and through forests—but saw no signs of them anywhere. Their disappearance worried everyone for days, but the marriage celebrations did their part in easing some of the pain.

Wolf Rider, meanwhile, grew more restless and homesick by the constant eating and dancing as the days wore on. Eventually, with eight horses in tow, he was escorted to the base of the mountains by his cousins, their husbands, Lone Elk, Ice Bear, and a party of Paducah warriors. Man Who Hunts the Moon shouted a cry of farewell and Wolf Rider saluted in return before leading his 'herd of riches' through a stream. As he crossed it, he kept dreaming of his success—

Eight giant wolves!

And a black bear robe!

The *Nabu'rac* have shown me favor!

That morning, under rain-soaked skies, he rode deeper into the forest toward Fire and Eagle Mountains. During that time, he thought about the horses and how they could help the tribe. With a herd of horses, he believed there were no boundaries where his people could go. What took days could now be done in half a day or less. Buffalo meat could be moved quickly for vast distances without spoiling. And speed was power. And power meant an advantage in battle. A war party could attack and retreat faster than the enemy could react. And buffalo hunts could be carried out quicker, easier, more efficiently, with better chances of success and less risk of injury. And having both mares and stallions assured the tribe of breeding more horses. And more horses meant more riches!

About two-thirds of the way home, however, that success was about to become threatened. Wolf Rider had a feeling he was being watched. As he took a drink from a pool beneath a waterfall, the forest grew quiet.

Too quiet.

He knew at once something was wrong. He looked to his left, then to his right, intent upon seeing the slightest shake of limb or stir of grass, but all throughout the land in front of him there was not a hint of wind or sound, except for the gentle tumble of water as it splashed down the creek bed.

Ahead, through a thicket of pines, he saw shadows moving. Giant Wolf neighed and rose up on its back hoofs while the rest of the horses bandied about nervously, tugging at the rope. Next, he heard rustling sounds, the scrape of moccasins across the forest floor. One Comanche after another was stealing closer within range of an arrow. He knew he could retreat and outrun them, but that would only show cowardice, so he teased them by yelling—

"Comanches, if you wish to ambush me, make no noise! You thunder about like buffalo!"

He waited. The footfalls stopped.

"Hear me!" he cried. "If you do not leave, I will let my giant wolves go. They will run you down! Eat you! Spit out your bones! And make widows of your wives!"

He listened. But again all he heard was the gentle flow of the water as it washed along the creek bed.

The silence angered him. He shrieked wildly, hysterically, then leapt onto Giant Wolf's back and kicked it into a mad gallop, pulling the horses down a narrow path.

Reacting quickly, Comanches warriors, in turn, sprang from the bushes and outlying forest in groups of two and three. From every direction he could hear arrows deflecting off of branches, striking tree trunks amid the frantic blare of war cries.

One attacker stood crouching on a tree limb. As the pounding hoofs drew closer, he jumped, only to land awkwardly on one of the horses. In desperation, he clung to its mane, trying to straddle a leg over its back. Wolf Rider struck him with the wooden side of his bow again and again until the attacker lost his grip and fell screaming under the weight of the crashing hoofs.

Deep into the woods Wolf Rider charged, the target of a never-ending barrage of arrows. The trees now worked in his favor, shielding him and the horses as they fled for their lives. The Comanches were closing in on three sides—front, back, and to his right. A party of braves raced to cut him off, scrambling down an embankment to get a better shot. Some of them scattered. The rest stood their ground, taking careful aim, releasing arrow after arrow as fast as they could nock them to their bows.

Wolf Rider clung to Giant Wolf's mane, leaning forward to make himself as small a target as he could. He kicked his heels into the animal's sides and could feel the stride of the powerful legs responding. The hoofs plodded over rock, through brush, hurtling forward as a storm of arrows hissed past. A shaft splintered. A mare went down, whinnying as she fell, the rope snapping. Three warriors leapt from the trees, positioning themselves directly in his path, and stood waiting with bows drawn, arrows pointing. The horses, however, came rushing at them with the relentless fury of a stampede. They were too quick and too strong and ran over them as their bodies hit the ground with a series of loud, bone-crunching thuds. Except for the mare, the rest of the herd struggled forward, when suddenly the arrows stopped. The clearing where the enemy stood was breached and Wolf Rider led the horses safely beyond, into a distant meadow.

He knew then the purpose of the attack was not to kill the horses. The arrows could have easily injured or destroyed the entire herd. Possession of the horses was what the Comanches wanted. In the end greed proved to be their undoing. With both arms raised, Wolf Rider leaned high on his mount and shouted a cry of victory.

He didn't have to look back to realize the extent of the damage done to the Comanches. He could hear the injured moaning. Nor did he escape without injury himself. An arrow had grazed his left leg, leaving a long gash just above the knee. Slowly, he dismounted, grimacing in pain, and examined each of the giant wolves. Two of them sustained minor wounds. Another had an arrow stuck in its flank and was limping badly. With the only Pawnee arrow spent in the skirmish, he mercifully took its life, then remounted, quietly saying a prayer to the *Nabu'rac*, praising the two dead animals and their brave spirits.

Angry yet confident, Wolf Rider rode home, vowed to a war that was certain to come.

He rode cautiously, aware of places in the thick underbrush, ridges, rocks, gullies, trees, wherever he could be ambushed and avoided them as best he could.

Before sunset, while crossing into the next valley, he pulled up suddenly and peered into the distance. Something caught his eye— something *fleshy* upon which four black crows were feeding. What he saw appeared to be out of place, at odds with the surroundings. Riding closer, he began to feel a sickness in the pit of his stomach. The crows, aware of the oncoming rider, cawed and flew away.

Suspended between two trees was a man dangling over the trail, his arms and legs outstretched, pulled taut against the ropes. His back was turned. He did not move. Blood, dripping down his leggings, had clotted onto the soles of his feet.

Aside from the condition, there was something ominous about the body hanging in the air. It was hung there for a purpose, as a sign, a warning to all who entered the mountains. Especially a Pawnee.

War Hawk had been made an example. He died in disgrace and shame, suffering the most hideous of tortures, his eyes removed, gouged by a knife in all likelihood while he was still alive.

A warrior who lost his eyes could never find his way into eternity, into the *afterlife*. Serenity would escape him forever—a cruel price to pay for being an enemy of the Comanche.

Wolf Rider did not have to see War Hawk's eyes to know what happened. He imagined it, which sickened him all the more. The smell made him gag and retch until, finally, he threw up.

* * *

He arrived home shortly before dusk. At first, everyone was thrilled to see the horses, but once they realized he rode alone, an uneasiness swept through camp, then anxiousness when they saw the heavy bundle draped over Giant Wolf's back, and finally shock as Wolf Rider lifted the bundle and placed it on the ground. Slowly, he rolled the bundle over, revealing a body wrapped in bearskin.

There was silence, revulsion, outrage.

Calmly, Wolf Rider explained what happened and identified the killers with a single word—

"Comanche," was all he said.

A groan cut through the crowd. A young woman named White Crow fell to her knees, sobbing, shaking, robbed of the man she had one day hoped to marry.

Later that evening, at his burial scaffold, a priest waved sacred feathers over War Hawk's body and repeated a chant over and over and ended it by saying, "Grandfather and all who have gone before us, take his spirit and make a place for him in the Shadow Land. Let him walk the winds and roam the sky where the spirits live. And may he rest as he sleeps in our hearts."

Everyone sang a Death Song. They grieved, allowing their hatred of the enemy to grow. It grew like a sickness through the Pawnee camp.

By the entrance to War Hawk's tepee, a sacred bundle was placed. A fire burned with branches gathered from the *waga chun*,* the Rustling Tree. White Crow wore a wreath in her hair of the 'sweet and cleansing sage.' She wailed, rocking back and forth on her knees while facing the fire. Behind her, dozens of others did the same, sitting sad and troubled by the Sacred Tepee—in honor of a respected warrior, a man who many believed could not be killed.

---

* holy tree, cottonwood

Adding further grievance to it all, the missing scouts, Black Eagle and Deer Slayer, were never found. Unfortunately, their families suffered the most, not knowing if they were alive or dead. In private they mourned, sometimes silently, sometimes not.

During a Council meeting, at the request of the chief, Wolf Rider spoke of his travels, commenting about the great Paducahs and treacherous Comanches. The details included his cousins' marriages and Lone Elk's and Ice Bear's adoptions into the Paducah tribe. The true purpose of the meeting, however, served to fuel the flames of hate, to talk of war, and avenge the taking of War Hawk's life.

Crammed inside the Council Lodge, warriors, priests, and chiefs listened as the war chief urged them on—

"From the green grass of *Tuh-parisu* to the peaks of the Shiny Mountains we have ventured. With each step we have taken, death has followed. If we are to die, let us die as *Wolf Pa'ni*, not as frightened children! The wicked ways of the Comanche must be silenced! Take courage, my brothers! Sharpen your knives! Tighten your bowstrings! And make ready for war!"

The Council responded with whoops and screams and cries, giving their approval.

A warrior wearing a bear-hooded headdress stood up. "The lives of ten men I will take!" he promised. And with an imaginary weapon, he mimicked the throwing of a spear.

Rattles shook and men shouted

"I will wash myself in blood," claimed another, "the blood of the Comanche!"

Louder the clamor rose.

"Death to the Comanche!" someone else cried.

A War Chant was echoed by all, ringing loud and far.

One by one, in the dim light of the tepee, men spoke of daring, of valor in battle, dedicating themselves to victory, and each time there was yelling and screaming and a shaking of rattles with an intensity never heard before.

Finally, with upraised arms, the war chief motioned for silence. He peered along the row of excited faces and said, "Fear not! It is the Comanche who will feel the might of the Pawnee! We will be cunning like a wolf...and strike like a snake!" He made a loud, hissing noise, imitating a diamondback, and everybody else did the same, followed by a deafening chorus of shouts and cheers as they worked themselves into a frenzy.

Afterwards, armed scouts were sent out to guard the village while preparations were made for a War Dance, a ceremony that hadn't been practiced for years.

Wolf Rider watched as a wooden scaffold was being erected in the middle of the dance grounds. He learned from Two Buffalo a woman had been taken captive during the raiding of an enemy village. She was to be executed at dawn, in observance of a ritual called the *Morning Star Ceremony*.

In keeping with tradition, the Morning Star priest forbid anyone to look at her. He placed her under guard outside the village. Wolf Rider, however, was curious about the woman. As soon as it was dark, he slipped past the sentries and spied the captive while hiding behind some bushes.

She was Comanche—very beautiful and young. Her clothes had been stripped from her and she was smeared in red paint from head to toe to symbolize torture and sacrificial blood. He was quite taken by her beauty and the way she conducted herself. She showed no signs of fear or worry, yet conveyed a sense of pride and innocence and something much deeper than that—a passion hidden, waiting to be lavished on the man she would wed. She did for him what Paw Dancer did for Man Who Hunts the Moon, only the young Pawnee was smitten more. She evoked a feeling in him he had never felt before. And for the rest of the night he resisted the celebration of the Morning Star Ceremony, just so he could gaze at her, Comanche though she was.

Chapter 9

On a quiet night
I can hear the moon glow
and the soft feathery feet
of a blue bird
as it alights on a cloud.

– Indian poem
origin unknown

THE CAPTIVE WAS TAKEN, shivering and cold, to the scaffold in the dead of night. She did not put up a struggle or again show any fear. The paint representing sacrificial blood was reapplied, after which she was tied to the wooden platform and treated with the highest respect.

While it was still dark, squaws and old men were the first to gather. They laid charms, jewelry, *pa'hut;** wampum, a whole host of things at her feet, so when she died, her spirit would be enriched with gifts in the afterlife. Soon a crier went through camp spreading the word that the Comanche was about to be sacrificed to avenge those who had been killed in battle.

One by one, men and women gathered around a large drum about as wide as a man was tall and, with voices filled with sadness, wailed and moaned to let the gods know that what was about to be done grieved them. Assisting priests then danced around her, summoning the ghosts and spirits of the dead to prepare a place in their world for another—

---

* a string of beads, a necklace

another who undoubtedly had divined her fate, yet so far displayed a courage usually reserved for the most fearless of men.

Clothed in a ceremonial shirt and long feathered headdress, the presiding priest beckoned to the Being of the Morning Star, facing east where the sun was about to rise. Over and over he recited words of encouragement for dawn to break, his arms outstretched, as if he had the power to influence it—

"Look afar! Born is the sacred light. Brave be the heart of the maiden child. Brave be the heart."

Aroused by the sleeping mist in the clearing, dogs barked mournfully while black squirrels chirred and the partridge and whippoorwill sang, ushering in the morning

Darkness was lifting, slowly, like water receding from a shore.

To begin the proceedings, three men took up batons and beat them slowly on the drum while the priest chanted and danced around the scaffold, a prayer stick in one hand and rattle in the other. The prayer stick he held steady, trying to implant Pawnee forces into the maiden. The second he shook. It rattled like a snake, poisoning, weakening her Comanche will.

Alongside him joined more dancers. The first was a bear, a man in costume—hide, head, hair, and all—with the chin of the animal resting against the crown of his skull. Next came a warrior cloaked in wolf skin, hair and head intact, body hunched over, giving the effect of walking on all fours. The third was a hawk, covered in feathers, wearing a long-beaked mask. The fourth and final dancer was an elk with buckskin shirt and full set of antlers. Together, the four danced in rhythm to the drum, hopping and skipping from one foot to the next.

Closer the sun rose to the east, unveiling a streak of pale light stretching across the rim of the horizon. And louder and faster came the drumbeats.

Amazingly, the Comanche woman stood unfazed by it all. She held her head high and looked beyond the restless crowd, concentrating on some place distant. Not once did she show a sign of breaking down or shedding a tear.

The camp, however, was astir with anticipation as a torch was cast into the fire pit. Murmurs swept through the crowd as the flames burst, flashing upward through a stack of wood, crackling fiercely, unleashing a torrid brilliance of crimson and gold. In the glare of the intense fire the wailing and moaning heightened, growing to a feverish pitch.

Nearer and nearer the sunlight came.

The Morning Star priest, in a voice that was hoarse and rough, shouted out the names of those who were killed in battle. He then asked the beasts of the grassy plain and birds of the sky, and their spirits, the *Nabu'rac*, to join in.

All that awaited was the execution.

What a frenzied spectacle it was!

The camp was ablaze in firelight. Seven priests in long, flowing headdresses danced. Around them danced the Bear, the Wolf, the Hawk, and Elk. And around them rose the tumult of the crowd, bodies swaying deliriously, throats raw from screaming, as the drum beat louder and faster—like pulses of thunder coming from the gods.

Amid the commotion a Death Skull, taken from a buffalo and bleached white, was laid at the maiden's feet.

People cried out as bowmen readied their arrows. Spirits and ghosts lurched throughout the campgrounds, converging on the platform.

The moment of the Morning Star was now poised.

With it, the first rays of sunlight appeared, shining along the eastern edge of the sky, changing from a pinkish gray to a bright radiance.

The priest raised his arm. "Behold the Star!"

The crowd fell silent.

Bowstrings were drawn, arrows pointing.

It all happened so fast. Hoof beats charged through camp, but were drowned out by the pounding of the drum. The Morning Star priest saw something moving swiftly out of the corner of his eye. As he turned, he was swept aside—in part by animal, in part by young warrior.

Startled eyes saw Wolf Rider leap from his horse and, with a knife, cut the Comanche loose. The bowmen hesitated, not knowing what to do. In the confusion, the drumbeats stopped. Musk Raven and Two Buffalo stood up in shock while all around them people shouted and gasped. Wolf Rider threw the maiden on Giant Wolf's back, then hopped on, and the two sped away before the first arrow was shot. A tremendous cry of rage and disbelief went up. Warriors started to give chase, but realized the futility of it.

Wolf Rider did not think of the consequences of what he had done and was only concerned with escape. So he rode—without care, without guilt, but with a sense of purpose—holding the Comanche woman firmly in his arms. Her glistening black hair, trailing in the wind, was all that he saw. She would not show her face.

Their escape led to a mountain bluff at the edge of the Shiny Mountains, a ride that lasted all morning. The bluff overlooked an expanse of rolling hills stretching to the flatlands to the east. There, along a ridge barren of trees, they camped—under a vista of blue sky, aspen, and pine.

He tried to talk to her, but she would not speak. Every attempt to win her confidence failed. Whenever he approached her, she would act disinterested and simply walk away. Finally, she stood unclothed at the edge of the bluff, back turned, body covered from her breasts to her knees in dried paint, oblivious to the wind and chill of the mountain air, staring off into the distance, as if she were resentful of him and the very act which had saved her life.

As for Wolf Rider, he had come to this place unprepared, having only a knife, bow, quiver of arrows, and bearskin to sleep upon. Little else in the way of necessities did he have. Yet he knew the High Country was fraught with danger. There was an element of the unknown here that made survival risky. Bear tracks and tracks made by mountain lions were in evidence everywhere, living proof that both creatures prowled the woods unceasingly day and night.

The Comanche woman had no weapon to defend herself with, so Wolf Rider cut down a branch from a tree. Using his knife, he sharpened the tip, trimmed the branches and bark from the shaft, and hurled the makeshift spear at her feet.

"There," he said. "Should a bear desire to make food of you."

In place of a dress he gave her the bearskin which provided warmth during the *Moon of the Ripened Corn* (September-October), and for the rest of the afternoon he went hunting with bow and arrow in search of food, not sure what the Comanche woman would do in his absence, or if she would be there when he returned.

To his surprise, she was kneeling by a fire when he rode up. Using a skill he did not know she had, she made a fire by rubbing two sticks together. In his own way, Wolf Rider proved to be quite resourceful as well. Hanging from Giant Wolf's neck was a string of rabbits and a pink-fleshed trout, the length of his arm, which he skinned, gutted, and slowly roasted over the fire…until the meat was tender, seared on the outside, succulent on the inside. For two people who had not eaten all day, it was a feast impossible to resist.

But resist she did.

Dangling a piece of cooked rabbit in front of her, he said, "Eat!"

She fought the temptation, however, lips pressed tight as she glanced indignantly away.

While he ate, she refused to break her silence, refused his offerings of food and bearskin as well, sitting naked, hugging her knees, showing no emotion whatsoever.

The silence made him uneasy. Guilt and worry began to fester and grow as he fell prey to doubt. Would his people forgive him? Would he be banished forever? Had he shamed his mother and father? What would he do with the Comanche? Return her to her village?

None of this he knew.

Somehow he felt he had no people, no home. Certainly he had nowhere to go, no respect for himself, and, more importantly, the woman he loved surely had no love for him.

He sat, staring at the fire, unable to eat.

At last, the Comanche wrapped herself in the bearskin and said, "When I was a child, my father told me of a place where spirits sing."

He raised his eyes to her.

She asked his name and the name of the beast he mastered, and she gave hers—*Cloud Wing*, a name given to her by her father because one night, as a young girl, she had a dream-vision of flying through the clouds as a bird, not just any bird, but a Great Blue Heron.

"I do not know how it is with Pawnees," said Cloud Wing. "But Comanche women can read faces and feel spirits. When a man is in darkness, he has no shadow. To return the man's shadow, he and others near him pray for light." Her tone was tender. The aloofness she maintained was now gone.

With a stick, she poked at the fire and continued, "Wolf Rider once helped me, so now I wish to help him. I know a place where he could find the shadow of himself. It is a long way from here—the *Home of the Ancients*, a great wide hole in the earth where man and animal first saw light. I could take you, but among the Comanches it is better for a man to seek his vision of light alone. If you wish, I will speak of the trail that leads to the *Sacred Hole*."

He nodded, encouraging her to go on.

"It is far beyond the mountains," she explained, "beyond the desert, where there is only rock and sand. No grasses. No trees. The gods have marked it. Two heads of stone rise high above the earth, almost touching the sky. To reach them, you must go through the mountains, around what is known as Dream Lake, along the River of White Waters, to first find the desert. But the journey is long and dangerous, especially where there is little food and no water. Once a person crosses the desert, he will see the Ancient Heads of Stone. Beyond lies the Sacred Hole. Good spirits and bad spirits live there, as do the *Makers of First Light*. If a man's prayers are good and he is deserving, the spirits will answer. The man will be filled with light and his shadow restored."

"But I do not think I could find this place," Wolf Rider replied.

"With Giant Wolf to take you and the trail marked by word pictures, you could. Just follow the River of White Waters…" She stopped and wrapped the bearskin around her shoulders, saying nothing more.

"Why have I never heard of this Sacred Hole?" he wondered.

"Maybe your people have forgotten how life began. Our fathers and great grandfathers—the *Ancients*—all came from there. It is the most sacred of all places, the Fertile Rock, Giver of Light, our Sacred Home. Just to see it gives one wisdom he could never possess."

"Why do you tell me this?" he asked.

"I see sadness in your face," said Cloud Wing. "What you did today was very brave. You honored me, but in your mind shamed yourself. Peace will not be found within you. It must come from some place else."

Wolf Rider thought for a moment and whispered, "I will seek a Vision of Light."

Flushed from the heat of the fire, Cloud Wing's silhouette danced and shimmered in a haze of drifting smoke. He stared at her, infatuated by the way her hair fell softly around her shoulders. By the innocence of her dark eyes. By everything about her.

He knew if she could feel spirits and read faces, his love of her was a mystery no longer.

"Now will you eat?" he asked, smiling.

When she smiled back, he felt a warmth glowing inside him.

After they ate, he gathered more wood for the fire while she drew the trail to the Sacred Hole on a piece of leather, using the charred end of a burnt stick to make the word pictures. Under a cloudless sky, they bedded down together side by side with Wolf Rider lying on the bare ground and Cloud Wing, opposite him, rolled in the bearskin.

A night owl hooted. A nighthawk screeched. A bear roared from a distant mountain.

They listened to the sounds of the night and talked. They talked about themselves, their families, their beliefs as they watched the stars and moon float gently above.

During the night Cloud Wing got up, covered him with the bearskin before stretching out alongside him—while Wolf Rider only pretended to sleep. Later, he did the same. He slipped the skin back over her and gazed at her face. But she, too, only pretended to sleep.

Chapter 10

WOLF RIDER RELIVED THAT NIGHT and following day many times throughout his journey. He pictured Cloud Wind as she waded, shivering, into the stream, bathing in the cold, cold water. He remembered how she gently washed the paint from her shoulders, her neck, her breasts, down to her knees, and then later, before returning home to her village, saying she hoped "the blood of war between our people will one day be cleansed." The recollection of her standing on the bank—the paint rubbed clean, her body shining, so lovely and inviting—kindled more than warmth. It started a fire within him. He recalled her last words when they parted as she hugged the bearskin robe around her:

"To the Bear and to the Eagle I will pray to make you strong. I will ask the Spirit Creatures of the West to protect you, to guide you safely through the mountains to the river. And to my father I will bare my heart. I will tell him this is a Pawnee's gift of peace. May you find the peace you seek, Wolf Rider."

He nodded and said nothing. Not aloud, anyway. But to himself he said, "And in my heart I will build a sacred fire, and through the day and through the night I will keep it burning. It will burn only for you."

Since that moment, he wondered if he would ever see her again.

Though now he rode alone, he carried the image of Cloud Wind with him wherever he went, as well as her crude map. From it, the trail to the Sacred Hole seemed simple enough, but the word pictures could not begin to show the severity of the lands he would cross. Passage through the mountains took more than persistence. To travel up and down slopes and through valleys took very deft hands, a strong back, good judgment, and dexterity on both his and Giant Wolf's part. Many times they had to create a path where no path had been.

And the constant uphill, downhill traversing wore on the legs of the animal as well as the backside of the rider. If the steepness of the terrain or congestion of the trees did not present a problem, a stream or river usually did.

Oddly, he saw almost no evidence of human life—a burned out campfire one time, tracks many days old another—but little else. The friendliness or belligerence of the mountain tribes, namely the Utes and Arapahoes, remained unknown. Nor did the reputed dangers of the mountain creatures create much of a problem. On occasion Giant Wolf was spooked by the sudden roar of a black bear or snarl of a mountain lion, but neither of them ventured close enough to pose a real threat. Among the other animals, however, he saw a wide variety, ranging from a beaver, deer, moose, fox, badger, ferret, and bobcat, which he had never seen before. Quiet, stout-bodied, with spotted fur and short, stubby tail—the bobcat crept along like a small panther, could run as fast as Giant Wolf, and was incredibly agile.

For three days Wolf Rider roamed through a succession of forested valleys until he came to Dream Lake, a cold, green sheet of melted snow where the trees thinned atop rocky cliffs and clustered around the lakeshore. From Dream Lake, half a day's ride, he found the River of White Waters. Currents foamed, churning down from mountain to mountain, rumbling over rocky chasms under swells of surging water. According to Cloud Wing's map, somewhere along the great river he was supposed to cross to the opposite bank, but throughout the High Country there was far too much turbulence to cross.

Several days later, during the *Moon When Calves Grow Hair* (October), the flow of the river began to subside and, with it, the mountains turned into hills, the hills into buttes, plateaus, and long stretches of scrublands, consisting of rock and hardened sand. At the same time the weather became warmer—so warm in fact, his skin burned from exposure to the sun. Yet he welcomed this new land, for it marked the first time he could let Giant Wolf run without restraint. No hills or trees to slow it down, just an even, smooth level of ground upon which its legs could canter in easy stride. Together they ventured through a plains, not of grass, but of dust, sand, and stone—the wind whipping through his hair and thrill of sights never seen before, which kept him distracted.

Throughout the journey Giant Wolf proved to be obedient and even tempered, displaying a remarkable willingness to take him wherever he wanted to go. Seldom did it take exception to the distances traveled or to the hardship of running and walking from sunup to dusk, day after day. Wolf Rider, meanwhile, was smart enough to realize when the animal was tiring, when it was hungry, or ready to trot at a more leisurely pace, and he quickly came to appreciate the habits and behavior of the horse. The position of its ears, for example, told him a great deal. If angled forward, it meant Giant Wolf was either curious, or suspicious. If angled back—nervous, shy, agitated, or simply afraid. If one ear was bent forward, the other back, it was uncertain. And when the ears stood straight up, the horse was contented, pleased, or had no negative feelings at all. How it positioned its head, its tail, the movements of its body, the sounds that it made—neighing, whinnying—all of these things communicated some aspect of its personality, and little by little he was able to gain a better understanding of it.

Early one afternoon, they came to a bend in the river of White Waters where the banks narrowed. From the river's natural flow, he estimated a person could set adrift from one bank, swim, or simply float, and pass to the other side without much effort. After checking conditions downstream, he returned to the first location, led Giant Wolf into the water and—while clutching its mane and floating on its back—he crossed to the opposite bank.

At that point, once again the terrain changed. The rock formations were flatter, the scrub bushes more sparse, and sand was compacted in layers and heaped in masses along a succession of broad, red-stone canyons. Every now and again, rising out of the plain, were sharp ridges and square-topped buttes, sometimes bare, sometimes marked by short, sturdy trees whose trunks were twisted, formed by the unceasing elements of nature.

Later that night, he experienced his first sand storm. No rain. Just wind. It hurled dust and sand so hard and thick, it stung his skin and blinded him. There was no sense in continuing on, so he made Giant Wolf lie under a shelter of rock and curled up beside it, closing his eyes. And soon the Dream-Maker was conjuring up a dream.

At sunrise, he dug his way out from under a blanket of sand which had settled during the night. Soon as he got up, he realized Giant Wolf was gone. Panicked by the thought of being stranded alone in a hostile climate, he ran to the top of the nearest ridge and viewed the land below. Nothing. Not a trace of his once-faithful horse. All he could see was an endless stretch of sun-baked desert, extending from canyon to canyon.

For a moment he almost conceded his death right where he stood. He noticed, however, the river was still within sight. He also had a knife and pouch full of *pimmican** to eat. Having no idea where or how far Giant Wolf may have wandered, he returned to the shelter of rock. There, he looked for tracks and found them embedded in the sand. They led in the direction he was headed—due west, *Where the Sun falls*—but the closer he got to the river, the stronger the wind blew and more difficult it was to see the tracks, until eventually there were no tracks at all, just a monotonous stretch of sand. Given the proximity of the river, he reasoned, the less the animal would stray, so he continued across the hot, empty desert within walking distance of the river.

His first day on foot comprised one simple task: to cover as much ground as he could, in search of Giant Wolf. Twice he walked to the river to satisfy his thirst. Otherwise, the day went without incident, except for a few sightings of coyotes and an occasional rest whereby he would nibble on granules of pimmican. The second and third days were a repeat of the first. He would run until he was tired, rest, walk to the river for a drink. Once there, he would bathe in the shallows to cool himself, then return to the desert in pursuit of the horse. At night his legs and back would ache from the strenuous pace, but in the morning, after running and walking a short distance, they would loosen up. By midday, however, the sun shined its brightest, glaring across the barren landscape, and the heat—the insufferable heat—forced lizards and snakes to find shelter under rocks, under crevices, wherever there was shade or the remote suggestion of shade. His legs and back would tire again and the cycle would repeat itself, only worse than before.

Blisters formed on his face from exposure to the sun...on the soles of his feet from the repeated poundings over the stone-hard sand. The Desert Country, meanwhile, remained constant. Each canyon was

---

* mixture of dried corn and meat

rimmed by a circular ridge of hills or short strip of plateaus spaced farther and farther apart. And each canyon became successively harder
and harder to reach.

By the fourth day of travel, he had used up all of his pimmican.
His feet were calloused, cracked, and blistered from heel to toe, his
moccasins torn and bare, and fatigue had long since become a steady
companion. Each period of rest and each trip to the river lasted longer and longer, and each time it took a little more strength of will and
determination to resume passage through the rough terrain. His stride
was no long graceful or swift. He hobbled and sometimes staggered,
yet somehow always found a way to remain on his feet. The wind, heat,
and sun exacted a terrible toll on him, far worse than he realized. The
farther he progressed, the more his mind drifted, lapsed into a feeble
state. There were moments when he couldn't remember anything, how
or where he had crossed a canyon, or even what it was that he was
pursuing. Sometimes the tracks he thought he was following were mo-
mentarily forgotten until, finally, he stopped for one of his now fre-
quent rests. After sitting for a while, relaxing, catching his breath, he
noticed two distinct formations looming above the horizon.

The Heads of the Ancient Warriors!

They rose up tall, great columns of rock, standing nobly against
the blue of the sky.

Wolf Rider sang out, laughing, and pushed himself as hard as he
could. He ran until he was exhausted, until cramps and fatigue were the
only feelings left in his legs. Countless times he stumbled and fell, skin-
ning his elbows and knees, only to crawl, get up, and stumble again. By the
time he reached his destination, he could barely walk, much less run. He
staggered through the corridor separating the Heads of Stone, delirious
and weak, yet gazed in wonder at their heights. Their sides were arched
and ringed with layers of sandstone, leading up to the twin abutting chins
that framed the bottom of the monolithic skulls. To him they were holy
symbols, images of the *Ancients*, very near to the heart of *Ti-ra-wa*,* apart
from other forms of mere rock. At their rim, the most magnificent shrine
to spirits lay exposed—the *Sacred Hole*!—the place where man and animal first saw light, an immensely wide, deep canyon.

He stood looking at it in awe. Dry river beds merged with rolling
basins, long ago eroded by massive, gouging bodies of water and ice.

Buttes and plateaus, perfectly flat on top and curved beneath with life-like figures of stone jutting throughout, sprouted at random from the canyon floor, all crafted as if by some ancient pottery-maker.

The great Hole glistened under the sun with golden clays and orange, red, and burnt-brown sandstones, effecting a wetness in an arid land. The colors sparkled so brightly and with such contrast, they seemed as if they had been painted on, perhaps by the Artists of the Early World, the Makers of First Light who lured the first of human-kind from their earthen womb when "*light was born.*"

Wolf Rider worshiped its beauty. It was everything Cloud Wing said it was. And more. He felt a host of spirits dwelling within its shadows. Every man, women, and child, he thought, should witness it, feel its powerful effect and pray to the ones who created it.

And as he worshiped, he knelt, calling to the spirits who lived there, when, suddenly, leaping at his back, came a large and powerful beast. It growled and lashed at him with thorn-sharp claws. The claws ripped down his shoulder and across his left side as the weight of its body threw him over. Pain and shock slowed his reaction. The creature turned and attacked again, swiping out, trying to gather him in the clutch of its teeth. Gashes opened along both of his legs. He kicked. The heel of his foot drove into the animal's neck, pushing it away. He reached for his knife. Back the creature sprang, fangs snapping, claws slashing. This time the skin along his hip and thigh tore, the blood spurting. Wildly, he stabbed. The knife cut its leg. There was a brief roar. The panther recoiled in anger, then hurled itself into his chest. At the same time Wolf Rider rolled to his feet. The blade of the knife came thrusting up to meet it. The knifepoint punctured fur, ripping deep into the stomach as they both glanced over the edge of the canyon wall. Their bodies rolled...tumbled together as a cloud of dust and loose rock accompanied them downward, somersaulting head over foot along a steep slope. One hundred feet to the base of the canyon floor they fell, dust and rock settling.

Neither man nor animal moved.

Wolf Rider finally squinted an eye open. The last thing he expected to see were the spirits of the dead gathering over him.

---

* Supreme Ruler, god of gods, the One Above

BOOK FOUR: WOLF RIDER
The Stone Shirt

Chapter 11

"...A blow to my head made my body go dead,
but my mind was still alive. I could hear words,
yet could not move. In the Shadow Land I lay..."

— from *Indian Days of Long Ago*
by Edward S. Curtis

THE SPIRITS NEVER GATHERED.

When Wolf Rider opened his eyes, he found himself stolen away inside a cave, immersed in a pool filled with mud and salt. The skin of a panther, the one he had killed, was hanging from antler horns anchored to the wall, its carcass skewered by a lance, suspended over a fire near the cave's entrance. Behind him, on the floor were four circles bordered in stone, each enclosing a sand painting of some kind. A large boulder bulged from a side wall and across the breadth of it crude figures were painted. Lining the face of the back wall, partly obscured by piles of scrub timber, were more drawings—of elk, deer, and buffalo—and a sequence of figures too ambiguous to identify.

Scattered about randomly were baskets woven from straw, pottery, skins, pelts, a drying rack, spears, tomahawks, bows, arrows, and assorted tools made from bone, wood, or stone. Obviously, whoever lived here was a hunter, a tool and weapon maker, basket weaver, and maker of pottery, a type he had never seen before, bearing complex designs and a high degree of craftsmanship.

As Wolf Rider leaned forward to stand, he noticed something stirring at opposite sides of him. To his right, a dog with one eye and a long, deep scar over his other eye raised its head and whined. To his left, an owl flapped its wings, jerked its neck this way and that, blinked, hooted, and settled back onto its perch, a wooden post sticking horizontally from the wall. Below it, several more posts rose incrementally from the floor, like steps.

The combination of pain and sudden emergence of an old man who poked him with a stick, sent Wolf Rider slumping back into the pool. His entire body, especially his legs and back, hurt so much, the pain prohibited movement of any kind and he was far too distressed by this to take notice of the old man, let alone his surroundings. Fact is, Wolf Rider could do very little in those first few days but lie in what he later came to know as '*the healing pool*' and wonder what was real and what in part he dreamt, for as soon as he was conscious, he would drift back into a heavy sleep again and again, only to have his sleep interrupted when it was time to be fed. The old man would slap him with a stick—not hard, not angrily, or out of meanness, merely to wake him up—then yell, "*Hee-ya! Hee-ya!*" and pry his mouth open and stuff it full, sometimes nearly choking him with a type of pinole mush.

Other than an occasional repast, their relationship consisted of little more. Neither of them spoke, but often imparted utterances, groans, or mumblings under their breaths. Finally, after long periods of silence, Wolf Rider attempted a conversation, several in fact, but the old man would play deaf, hum, sing, talk to himself, talk to the one-eyed dog, or make strange cooing sounds as if speaking to the owl while feeding it. Or, he kept busy with odd little chores.

A strange little man he was—slight of build, dressed in animal skins and gray fur coat, with narrow, stooped shoulders, arms perpetually bent at the elbows, and long, stringy hair the color of a winter sky that fell haphazardly to his shoulders. A necklace of blue stones hung from his neck and jangled when he moved. When he walked, he took choppy little steps. And his sharp, penetrating eyes were always flashing this way and that when he was thinking.

One day, apparently convinced the young man had recovered long enough, the old man brandished his stick once again, slapping it intentionally harder, more vigorous than before. It stung. Wolf Rider flinched and complained, but was beaten, coaxed out of the pool, out of the cave where he was scrubbed clean and made to lay on a blanket in the sunlight, so his wounds would congeal and heal more quickly.

After a full day in the sun, the old man returned to inspect one of the cuts. He tapped his stick over a scab and to his surprise Wolf Rider felt no pain at all. The old man grinned, pleased by his medicines skills, and for the first time spoke, inquiring with a single word—

"Pawnee?"

"Yes, Pawnee," Wolf Rider replied. "You?"

The old man answered, *"Dine."**

Thus began what was a long and difficult exchange. Their languages, while sharing common origins and common traits, were somewhat different. They communicated as best they could through a series of signs and words translated into the others' tongue. Once they found expressions familiar to both, with patience and practice they talked in a kind of language derived from each.

The old Navajo claimed his reason for not speaking had to do with the process of healing. He said talk poisoned the spirits within a mending body, whereas silence had the opposite effect.

Later, over a meal of panther meat, they discussed the customs and culture of their respective tribes, but very little of their private lives. The young Pawnee avoided any mention of Giant Wolf or why he was separated from his people. He soon learned, however, the Navajo's name was *Secret Pipe* and during the course of his recovery Wolf Rider realized how well it suited the old man, for Secret Pipe was often brooding, smoking his pipe, preoccupied with his paintings, or gone from the cave engaged in some secret activity.

One night while he was alone, Wolf Rider took the opportunity to study the sand paintings more closely. All were similar in style, with bold swirling lines connected along the outer edges, outlining what appeared to be a hawk or thunderbird, a cornstalk, and cluster of stars. The painting on the boulder, however, proved to be the most interesting in that it portrayed a war between two opposing tribes. The first was in retreat afoot while its warriors tried to fend off the attack of a second tribe whose warriors, sitting astride giant wolves, carried sticks instead of bows. What made the sides so dissimilar was not the presence of the sticks or the horses, but the coloration of the people. One was red, the other a pale yellow. Intrigued by this, Wolf Rider stared

---

* Navajo, meaning folk, people.

at each figure, trying to understand the implications of the story, but grasped little of it, other than it was a war painting of some kind.

The next night as he and Secret Pipe were walking about the Sacred Hole, the subject of the paintings came up. Inspired by the brightness of the evening, the Navajo said he was a shaman and painter of the *Dine Star Cult*. He revealed that the Beings of the Other World, the gods and spirits, traveled from the sky to earth and back again upon rainbows, lightning, and by way of the sun and the moon. He explained that by tracing stars and particular star clusters he could perceive the bodies of the heavenly spirits who lived up high. His paintings, therefore, were simply interpretations of those perceptions.

Wolf Rider listened carefully and asked many questions about the Dine and what specific star clusters meant before pursuing the most pressing question of all—

"What is the meaning of the war painting?" he asked.

Secret Pipe reached down, petted the dog, and said, "I am glad you killed the panther. One Eye is glad, too."

Not satisfied by the answer, Wolf Rider addressed the issue again— "The people—why are they fighting?"

Secret Pipe's face turned suddenly grim. "It is not for you to know," he said.

* * *

By the time his wounds had healed, Wolf Rider was ready to seek a Vision of Light. Even though it was now *Moon of the Heavy Snows* (January), snow seldom fell in the canyon. To prepare for his vision, he went without food and water during the day and ventured out into the gorge that night. There, by a fire he sat, stripped of his leggings and shirt, humbly exposed to the Makers of First Light, quietly confessing to the incident that outraged his people, deprived him of his shadow, and led indirectly to the loss of Giant Wolf.

"Come, *Nabu'rac*," he said. "Come help the boy you once knew as Flying Fox. He camps with you now…in the Sacred Hole. He is a fool, I know, but the Comanche woman did nothing to harm the Pawnee. Why should she die for what her people did? If I was wrong, take my life. If I was right, sing me a song. Tell the Makers to give me light…"

Again, as he did once before, he purged himself of every wrong and renounced every foolish act he had ever done as a child, or as a man, and as he atoned for himself, the moon shone bright and full on the great canyon, highlighting the massive formations of rock, bathing each ridge, each bluff with a clarity seldom seen at night.

It wasn't until sunup that Secret Pipe realized the sleeping mat against the far wall was empty. When he finally located the Pawnee's whereabouts, he did not interfere. Instead, he made periodic checks throughout the day, occasionally slipping close enough to overhear parts of a prayer. After a while, he realized the young Pawnee was seeking forgiveness for a grave misdeed. The exact crime, if crime it was, Secret Pipe did not know. But, piece by piece, he found out how, why, and by what means the young brave had come to the Sacred Hole—riding, as he understood it, on the back of an animal known as "*Giant Wolf.*" And the more Secret Pipe learned, the more respect he had for his young friend.

For three days and nights Wolf Rider never strayed from his purpose. He withstood the elements and chill of darkness, always open for a sign, a vision, while pleading to the spirits for forgiveness. The soreness of his body came and went with the passing of time, as did the want of food and water. He suppressed each need, each desire by the sheer power of his will, ridding his mind of useless thoughts while conquering weakness by believing he was strong. And strong he was. During those moments when he thought he could tolerate no more, he would find new strength and overcome the pain. When hunger and thirst seemed unbearable, he would think of something else or refocus his efforts on the task at hand. Each time, however, it became harder and harder to concentrate.

Eventually, after a great deal of inactivity—sitting, waiting, and praying—he began to experience a light-headedness, which led to mild hallucinations. By day, the reflection of the sun shimmered over the landscape, evoking images of rivers and lakes, yet somehow he knew these were not the visions expected by the Makers of First Light. At night, his imagination saw what the eye did not. Shadows seemed to move about—passing behind boulders, beneath cliffs and ledges, skulking everywhere beyond the fringes of sight. Yet again he considered these mere apparitions—ghosts. And for every hallucination imagined, he would gravitate back to the pain. Pain in the joints of his legs from sitting far too long. Pain in his back, neck, shoulders, all in support of his body…in the muscles, bones, and portions of his skin where the sun had beaten down, making it tender and red. Pain so severe he could no longer dismiss it—until finally he had weakened so much he could barely sit at all.

Back and forth he slipped in and out of consciousness. When awake, a certain kind of languor took hold of him, swept him under its spell. He was half alert one moment, barely the next, or wavering somewhere in between.

As day broke upon the fourth day, exhausted, hungry, thirsty, and knowing he had no strength left to give, he realized he had done everything he could to bring about a true vision, but one thing. Torture. Now it was necessary, he told himself, for all else had failed. Slowly, he took his knife. With eyes blinking into the glare of the sun, he lifted his arms, imploring the spirits to take pity on him. As he pressed the blade of the knife to his chest, he cried out in a trembling voice—

"Hear me, *Nabu'rac*! Hear me, Makers! Come show Wolf Rider! His shadow he wants! The fool can do no more than this…"

The knife blade slashed across the skin, cutting it. His chin slumped against his chest.

"If you want his death," he muttered, "then have it!"

His eyelids slowly closed. His body fell limp, collapsing, as sleep overpowered him.

Chapter 12

"It does not matter where the body lies,
for it is grass, but where the spirit is,
it will be good to be."

– Black Elk
from *Black Elk Speaks*

SLOWLY, LIKE A TIDE RISING FROM OBLIVION, he emerged from a state of unconsciousness—

His body was dead, but his mind was still alive. He could hear sounds, but could not move. In the *Shadowland* he lay…

There was no sun, no moon, only a dark haze where the Thunder Beings lived. No ground, no walls, no canyon. Only the feeling that he was drifting in air—alone.

Above him, lightning flashed. Giant wolves galloped with crashing hoofs. And thunder shook the sky again and again.

Below, in a valley, campfires burned. Amid the fire and smoke there were ghosts, moaning and singing a Song of Death. And in the center of a village there was a skin-covered lodge, over which hung a roof of cloud. Inside, his mother and father were slouched over a sick boy, and the boy was slowly sitting up.

The image faded as a hand touched his face. He smelled ash, something bitter, smoky, almost sweet. His eyes fluttered open—

In the daze of his first waking moments, Wolf Rider could hear the unmistakable sound of a rattlesnake, coiled and poised to strike. Gone were Musk Raven and Two Buffalo. Instead, two beady eyes were staring back at him. The sound he heard was no snake, but a medicine rattle and the person shaking it was an old man with long gray hair and gnarled, calloused hands.

Again, Wolf Rider found himself lying inside the cave next to a fire, over which lizards and small birds were being cooked. And again, he was laid-up, incapacitated, because of injury, this time self-inflicted. A scab had formed along his chest, covered by a thick gooey substance, resembling sap. Wolf Rider pointed at himself, made a gesture of sleep, inquiring how long had he been sleeping, and Secret Pipe held up three bony fingers, indicating *three moons*. When asked of the medicine that was applied to the cut, the old Dine stated proudly it was comprised of berries, the blood of a panther, boiled sagebrush leaves, fat rendered from buffalo meat, grease from antelope hoofs, and three or four other ingredients.

Slumping against a bed of fur, Wolf Rider sighed in disappointment. His heart was cold and sick. His eyes, lifeless. Though by no means did he regret being alive, his disappointment stemmed from not having a vision, and the prospects of receiving one did not appear any brighter in the near future.

For the next few days his mood did not change. Secret Pipe came and went, preparing food while keeping the fire burning, and little by little Wolf Rider braved the cold by walking around, gaining some much needed strength. During that time, they seldom talked, yet Secret Pipe observed that when the young Pawnee walked, he shuffled his feet. There was a pronounced slouch in his shoulders, a look of self-pity in his eyes.

To a certain extent Wolf Rider did, of course, feel sorry for himself. However, this condition grew more out of boredom than anything else. When Secret Pipe was away—often he was gone all morning or all afternoon, on two occasions both—Wolf Rider occupied himself by studying the sand paintings and figures painted on the walls of the cave. Of particular interest was a scene involving scores of men in canoes, in pursuit of a giant fish—a fish so big, it had to be seven times the size of the canoe. Because he did not understand the sand paintings or the figures, he grew more and more despondent.

Confused and dejected, he felt there was no reason to live. Even the spirits refused to take his life. He was a small, shadowless man who disgraced his family, dishonored his people, and failed not only himself, but failed Cloud Wing and the Makers of First Light.

So he decided to return to the place where he had sought his Vision of Light and once again knelt beside a fire upon the floor of the canyon as a full moon, the Evening Star, shone brightly. Taking his knife in both hands and pointing it towards himself, he whispered—

"Hear me, Makers! I call to you a last time. Wolf Rider lived a good life until he became a man. And since becoming a man, he has brought shame to himself and shame to his people. He gave his shadow for the love of a woman. He knows now it was a selfish thing to do…"

Suddenly, there was a stirring in the air. A huge, dark-winged bird swooped and shrieked, making the call of an eagle. It glided, making a smooth, effortless turn and disappeared. To his right he heard a squeal, no doubt the helpless cry of some small animal. Soon a fox came trotting by with a limp rodent clutched in its mouth.

"Ah, to be clever like a fox," he heard someone say. Beside a boulder to his right stood Secret Pipe, and squatting at his heels, the one-eyed dog. The Dine walked closer, gazing at the sky, and remarked, "My father once said, 'If someone knows how to catch an eagle without hurting it, he is wise beyond his years.'"

Secret Pipe studied the heavens for a moment, then thrust out an arm, pointing. "Look! A shooting star!" When the star faded, he added, "A great and powerful man, a man of medicine, once told me a story of how the stars came to be. Would you like to hear it?"

Wolf Rider nodded.

"In the early days," Secret Pipe said, "before there were stars, the Mother of our Land, the *Dine-tah*,* made a fire, and over the fire she cooked many things—buffalo, rabbit, deer, eagle, fox—and of the things she tasted these were her favorite. From the buffalo she took strength and courage. From the rabbit, nourishment to sustain life. From the eagle, the keenness of sight. From the deer, swiftness and agility. And from the fox, cleverness to survive in the wild.

"After she ate, she threw the bones back into the fire, and while inside the fire, the bones grew red-hot and became sparks, magical specks of light that flew skyward and stuck high against the night sky. And there they have remained to this day—spirits of the buffalo, rab-

---

* Land of the people

bit, eagle, deer, and fox—glowing beside the Spirit of the Great Father, all spread out above Earth Mother to watch over the *two-leggeds, four-leggeds*, and *wings-of-the-air*.

"And that very same man, the storyteller, the Maker of Medicine, also said what makes the *two-leggeds* different from all others is, a *four-legged* will eat another *four-legged*, yes? A *wing-of-the-air* will eat another *wing-of-the-air*, will it not? But, no *two-legged* shall eat another *two-legged* unless he has no spirit."

Secret Pipe raised a bony finger, shook it, and said, "I have known men who eat flesh. *Human* flesh. Myself, I cannot do such a thing. But a dog...?" With his hand, he patted his belly, made a noise like a hungry dog, and glanced down at One Eye.

Guilt-ridden and feeling more pathetic than ever, Wolf Rider slowly slid the knife back into its sheath. He wondered...not so much about the two-leggeds, the four-leggeds, or what was said, but rather what was *not* said: '*how do you catch an eagle without hurting it.*' As he turned to ask a question, the old man had already vanished into the night.

The next morning, while sharing a meal of cooked rabbit, Secret Pipe noticed Wolf Rider kept glancing at the figures painted on the back wall. "There is a place far from here," he said. "The *Great Water**..."

Using *hand talk* and a language common to both the Navajo and Pawnee, Secret Pipe described a place where men and women wore robes made from the bark of trees, where forests grew to the edge of the Great Water, and canoes were cut from tree trunks, hollowed out and used for fishing. "Water lashes like thunder at the rocky cliffs," he said. "And far from shore you can hear the cry of a Monster Fish. Let me tell you of this place..."

Secret Pipe explained that, although he was born a Navajo, he lived with many other tribes—Paiute, Chinook, Bella Coola, and later the Sioux. As a young man, he and his father often went hunting together. One day, while hunting in a place called Dead Deer Creek, Paiutes attacked them, his father was killed and Secret Pipe was taken captive as a slave. From the Paiutes to the Chinooks he was sold, leaving one life of misery for another. Eventually, he was traded to a dark-skinned

---

* Pacific Ocean

people in the Land of Deep Winter Snows, a people called the *Bella Coola* and the Bella Coola lived along the coast in wooden lodges and hunted throughout the Great Water.

"Fish of many kind are the food of the Bella Coola," Secret Pipe said, "and the greatest fish of all is a Monster as big as a hundred buffalo."

Wolf Rider stared, wide-eyed, in rapt attention, listening to every word.

"The first time I saw a Monster Fish I could hardly speak," Secret Pipe said. "To kill this Monster Fish, what the Bella Coola call a *whale*, is very hard work. And only great men...brave men can do it. But, first, the chief who leads the hunting party may be gone for days in the forest, singing and praying, so that the spears may be thrown straight. Sometimes all the hunters go to the forest to make their bodies pure.

"Then, as night changes to day, many canoes are taken out into the Great Water. But only the most skilled hunters carry a spear. The cutting point is a shell ground to a sharpness. The shell is held to the shaft by the gum of a pine. Rope, taken from the bark of a tree, is fastened to a spear. Attached to the rope are many floats made from the skin of an animal that lives in the Great Water. The name of this animal is called the *hair-seal*, and both it and the whale live in water so cold, if you and I swam in it, we would freeze and die.

"After paddling far from shore, sometimes the hunters would sit all day in canoes, sometimes all night, waiting for a whale to come. Sometimes, instead of a whale, a storm would come and toss the canoes up and down, up and down, and the men would fall over the sides and freeze before we could get to them. Sometimes, when the water was calm, we would tell stories, or just sleep. At night, we could hear the whales splashing...crying like a child."

To mimic it, Secret Pipe let out a soft cry, ending with a high-pitched, "*Ooooooo!*"

"If a whale was seen," he continued, "the hunters would paddle as fast as they could until they got close enough to spear it. If the whale sank or went deep, they would wait until it surfaced, then throw more spears into it. I have seen as many as sixteen spears sticking in a Monster Fish and countless floats to weaken it, but it takes most of day to accomplish such a feat. While pursuing it, hunting it, and killing it, all the men would sing songs in praise of its spirit, and pray that it would not be angry. Once the whale was dead, the work was just as hard to get the Monster Fish back home.

"Pulling something that big, weighing as much as a hundred buffalo, is tiring. Few men have the strength to do it. Many times I have seen hunters pass out after a full day of paddling."

Secret Pipe described the hunting of a whale further by saying a Monster Fish with a great "*humped back*" made tall waves when it splashed, waves that swept over the canoes and threw hunters over the sides to their deaths. Sometimes, a whale "would turn on an angry sea, rise beneath us, and strike the canoe with its head" and the men would either freeze or drown, or "…scream while being chewed by the Monster Fish…like you or I chew a piece of meat." The thrill of the chase, he added, was like no other experience. "And the celebration afterward, once the Monster Fish was cut up and cooked…" Pausing, he grinned that crooked, half toothless grin of his, and said, "There was much merry-making, feasting, dancing, and in our hearts much joy."

Wolf Rider just sat there, amazed. The thought of such a creature made the scene on the wall all the more fascinating. He asked question after question, devouring every bit of information he could. No description of the Monster Fish was good enough, no insight satisfying. For every explanation there were two or three inquiries as to the nature of the beast, the men who hunted it, and the Great Water.

"Tell me about the hair-seal?" asked Wolf Rider.

Secret Pipe took a deep breath and said, "It is about as big as a baby buffalo, has whiskers on his face, and swims by using his flippers and tail. When the sun shines, it lies sleeping on the rocks by the water. When you hunt it, you must walk quietly before shooting it." Secret Pipe made the gesture of a bow and arrow. "Sometimes a hunter will strike it with a club, stab it, or throw a spear at its heart. The seal is too swift and too smart to kill while it is swimming." He smacked his lips, saying, "And the meat is tender…as is the meat of a fish called a *salmon*."

"Salmon?"

"Yes, there is no fish like it."

He went on to describe how a salmon could jump, fling itself into the air, against the tide of a fast-moving river, and how no other fish could equal its size or spirit, except for the huge fish that swim in the Great Water.

"And this Great Water you speak of," Wolf Rider wondered, "is it as big as a river or a lake?"

Secret Pipe stretched his arms wide, "No, bigger! Much, much bigger! No one has gone from one side to the other. And when the water touches a wound, it burns! The tide rises and falls, crashing like thunder. I have seen waves as tall as the tallest tree. During a storm, it rages like an angry beast. Like *Yietso!*"*

Finally, when Secret Pipe had explained just about everything he could, Wolf Rider asked him how a Navajo slave ended up in a place where man and animal first saw light.

"The journey from there to here was a long one," said Secret Pipe. "I am tired. Perhaps some day I will tell you."

There was something in the look of his eyes—an expression of someone hurting, haunted by his past.

For now, Wolf Rider knew it was useless to ask.

Like himself, Secret Pipe had no shadow. And Wolf Rider was committed to finding his, or learning what Secret Pipe had done to lose such a vital part of himself.

---

* mythical beast of evil

Chapter 13

DESPITE TALES OF INTRIGUE, of Monster Fish and tribes he had never heard of, Wolf Rider's mood began to worsen. Plagued by prolonged bouts of lethargy, he slept late and often and kept to himself. Because of it, Secret Pipe grew increasingly worried. Many times he asked Wolf Rider if he was sick, "filled with dark spirits." Wolf Rider would remain silent or wander off to some remote place in the canyon to sit and pray. Or he would become restless and explore areas he had never been before. One such place was the dark recesses of the cave where the old man spent much of his time—doing what, Wolf Rider did not know. But he intended to find out.

Carrying a lit torch, he entered a passageway buried deep in the bedrock and followed it for fifty steps or so until it opened to a wide-yawning cavern with a smooth sloping floor, interrupted occasionally by sharp rocks that protruded upward, crushed between much bulkier formations, probably during the upheaval of a massive earthquake. The first thing he noticed was the musty odor and figures painted on the ceiling—the dominant one being a spider, *Spider Woman*, who acted as guardian of the cavern. She was surrounded by a constellation of stars. To his right, exposed in the trembling torchlight, lay a pile of scrub timber, enough to burn for many winters. Not lacking in food, water, or wood, Secret Pipe was proving to be far more resourceful than his frail condition was letting on.

What impressed Wolf Rider the most, however, was the size and depth of the cavern. The arched ceiling rose high above him, making the existence of the paintings even more puzzling. How did the old man paint on a ceiling so high?—he wondered.

As he listened, he could hear a faint drip, drip, drip of moisture from ceiling to floor and knew from experience where there was water in all likelihood there was food. Sure enough, after a quick investigation, he found patches of mushrooms sprouting from the floor, in basins, and along the outer edges of the walls. Farther ahead, beyond the reach of torchlight, there was a slow hissing sound as well, a steam or gas escaping from a fissure. The smell of sulfur, while not overpowering, caused his eyes to tear and throat to gag. After carefully stepping over and around crevices and rocks, coughing, blinking, and wiping the wetness from his eyes, he reached a mass of bedrock stretching as far as the light could carry.

Here and there, he could see clouds of vapor rising from cracks in the floor and, beyond, passages leading off in several directions, possibly into other caverns where underground springs once existed. Tucked in a far corner to his left, he noticed a scattering of bones and furs of animals of various colors and sizes, either resting on drying racks or lying in stacks. Opposite that was a mat for kneeling which faced an alter of sorts, burnt-out torches buried in the sand, a tanned hide with odd zigzag designs painted across it, stretched and attached to another drying rack, all of it near a campfire long since dead. Having seen enough, Wolf Rider returned to the cave.

Within a few days, once his cut had healed enough to permit it, he began to explore other parts of the canyon. He found bushes and stunted trees growing throughout the gorge—chokecherry, sage, willow, fir, and pine—and an assortment of reptiles and animals nesting among the vegetation, along crevasses, or in caves prevalent everywhere. During these explorations, he encountered everything from muskrats to snakes, lizards, bats, several species of foxes distinguished by color—red, gray, and black—and a long-eared pigmy fox.

Eager to prove his prowess as a hunter, he set out early one morning with a full compliment of weapons, only to return late that evening without a kill of any kind. The day was spent in frustration in search of Big Horn sheep which Secret Pipe said lived along the slopes of the upper canyon. Considering the survival instincts of the Big Horn, Wolf Rider's failure had less to do with ability and was more a matter of inexperience, not knowing the Big Horn's traits, habits, tendencies, and the fact that it could climb rocks better than any other living creature. The proof of it came the following morning when Secret Pipe struck out before daylight and returned a short time later with a young ram slung over his shoulders. When Wolf Rider woke up, the air was filled with the savory smell of mutton, dusted with sage, slowly roasting over the campfire. The aroma was too tempting to resist, though it only served to remind Wolf Rider that, as a hunter, he had much to learn.

Having glutted themselves with the meat of the Big Horn, they settled into a quiet existence until, finally, one day it rained, not hard, but a constant drizzle, combined with intermittent flakes of snow. It was a type of day where a person sought shelter and the comfort of a warm fire, and that was exactly what they did.

One Eye was curled beside the fire, asleep. The owl sat contentedly on its perch, cooing, while Secret Pipe fed it dead mice. From his sleeping mat Wolf Rider gazed absently at the falling rain. By late afternoon the rain had stopped. They soon received a visit from members of a wandering tribe called the Yuma. The Yumas were very friendly and related in custom and language to many of the neighboring tribes, including the Navajo. There were twenty men, women, and children in all, clothed in rabbitskin, each of whom pulled sleds made of poles, upon which sticks and branches were stacked.

Secret Pipe welcomed them with open arms as he would family. He offered them water, stew made from mutton, a place to sleep if needed, but the Yumas were very respectful, proposing a trade instead. In exchange for firewood, they wanted pottery and baskets. And of course Secret Pipe was quite willing to accommodate them. Most of the time was spent joking, sharing a pipe, smoking *chacun sha-sha,* the bark of the red willow, and exchanging stories.

The chief of the Yumas, a man with a quick easy smile, smoked constantly and the more he smoked, the more he would laugh. Once the trading was done, he embraced Secret Pipe, then Wolf Rider and remarked how pleased he was to meet the "son of a great man."

The rest of the Yumas soon followed, addressing Secret Pipe and Wolf Rider as if they were related, nodding and patting them on the shoulders, genuinely glad to meet them. Sometimes it felt like there were sixty Yumas, not twenty.

Afterwards, there was a big celebration. Women sang. Men took up sticks and, in the absence of drums, beat them on the rocks and floor. Together, with sticks pounding and voices raised in merriment, music went echoing throughout the cave.

"Come dance with us!" cried the Yuma chief to Wolf Rider.

All at once, two young maidens stepped forward. Grinning, they dragged him to his feet.

"Sing!" yelled the chief.

Soon everyone was singing and dancing and having a good time.

When the celebration was over, Secret Pipe was given a shiny coat of rabbitskin. Judging from the smile on his face, he hated to see the Yumas leave. In their honor he wore the coat, warm and snug inside it, as they loaded their goods and moved on.

Two days later, a scene having vastly different results would take place. It happened during a cold winter afternoon. Again One Eye was curled comfortably by the fire, sleeping. Secret Pipe was hunched over a piece of pottery, shaping it, rolling wet clay across a flat piece of stone. Wolf Rider was lying on his bed mat, staring at the ceiling, daydreaming of Cloud Wing. Lately, she was all he could think of. He had never known anyone to have such a deep and lasting effect on him. Filled with secret urges and passionate desires, he was heartbroken by the thought of never seeing her again. At night he could not sleep. In the morning he had no desire to get out of bed. And with each passing day the sadder he became. Nothing seemed to excite him any more. As the rain and snow fell, he could feel a vast and numbing depression coming over him. As he often did, he closed his eyes to escape the hopelessness of it—

When, suddenly, the owl cooed, "*A-hoo. A-hoo.*"

One Eye raised its head and barked.

Everyone listened. Outside, in the gorge, there was a sound of something scraping. It was so faint it could have been mistaken for the wind. One Eye growled, leapt to its feet, and went running out the cave, barking. Wolf Rider stood up, but Secret Pipe placed a finger to his lips. "Hide!" he whispered, and gestured to the back of the cave.

Wolf Rider ran to the passageway leading to the cavern. Pausing at the mouth, he peered back and could hear the scraping sound coming closer. As far as he could tell, sticks were being dragged through sand. There was something else, too—a clinking of something hard and hollow.

Without warning, war cries shattered the silence.

One Eye retreated, yelping, with its tail between its legs…as rocks and stones ricocheted off the canyon floor, nearly striking it. Secret Pipe hurried outside, raised his hands, pleading to several people not to harm the dog and was soon was surrounded by a party of angry looking Indians, led by a chief wearing a long feathered headdress. Wrapped in a pale ermine coat, decorated with beads and leather sashes, was a man of intimidating size and looks, with gnashing teeth, bent nose, and piercing eyes that glared from a face painted from chin to jaw in black. From his belt hung an assortment of ghastly, gory skulls, and fetishes of bleached bones that rattled when he moved.

Behind him was another chief who wore streaks of war paint and a bonnet of buffalo horns, and to both sides of him stood a handful of warriors outfitted in leather and fur, having a single feather or cluster of feathers sticking from their hair as they dragged sleds made of poles, packed with the bloodied remains of butchered sheep.

The chief regarded Secret Pipe as he would an enemy, leering at him with contempt. He spoke a language Wolf Rider had never heard before, talking rapidly with a tone of superiority, and motioned for the men to enter. Secret Pipe objected, but was chastised, then threatened. He watched helplessly as the chief walked into the cave toward the sand paintings. One by one, he ground his heels in each, kicking and disturbing the sand with his feet.

Pointing here and there, the chief shouted an order. He repeated it again and again. The men took up their tomahawks and slashed at everything in sight—baskets, shields, pottery. Nothing was overlooked. Buffalo hides, blankets, pelts, a basket of grain and basket of corn were taken, not out of need, but out of spite, including the panther hide, which hung from a drying rack.

In the heat of things, the owl made a crucial mistake. It hooted. The chief said something to Secret Pipe and Secret Pipe answered by saying the bird had a broken wing. In essence, he said it could not fly. Which was the wrong thing to say. The warriors threw rocks and stones at it, but the owl, in one great leap, tried to escape. It lifted itself, broken wing and all, and fluttered to the back of the cave, only to be shot down by an arrow.

Under a rain of feathers, it died before it struck the ground.

Everyone laughed, but Secret Pipe. He stared in shock—angry and crushed—his jaw hanging open. Through it all, he never moved, never made a sound, merely sat, eyes staring at the back of the cave.

Like greedy children, the men gathered tools, weapons, clothing, whatever they could find, including a shiny coat of rabbitskin, and returned to their sleds. The chief, meanwhile, lingered by the fire, warming his hands. He eyed a sleeping mat against the far wall with suspicion, then the mat closer to the fire.

He asked a question.

Secret Pipe responded meekly, without raising his head.

The chief stared silently at the interior of the cave, listening, studying the shadows from wall to wall.

Wolf Rider could feel his heart pounding. He knew if he was found out, something bad would happen to him, or to Secret Pipe. All he could hear was a jingle of skulls…and bones rattling.

The wicked chief swaggered back and forth in a threatening manner. Finally, he pointed at a boulder and asked about the war painting. Of particular interest were the figures painted in pale yellow. Secret Pipe did not answer, so the chief asked the question again. Still, there was no answer. Enraged, the chief whirled upon Secret Pipe and struck him hard across the cheek with the back of his hand, then shouted the question once more. Quietly, Secret Pipe recoiled from the force of the blow. He said something under his breath, at which time he was struck down yet again. And once more, it took a moment for the Navajo to recover. As he did, he groaned—

"*Wasichus.*"

Slowly, the chief drew back with a worried look on his face. Secret Pipe mentioned *Wasichus* a second time, then followed with an impassioned speech, filled with vague references and mysterious inflections.

Apparently, the word *Wasichus* carried a powerful meaning, one that struck fear in the heart of the chief.

Unsure what to do, he glared at Secret Pipe and kicked at a pot warming by the fire, the contents spilling, hissing against the embers. He uttered a short burst of words, then strode angrily away, his headdress sweeping behind him, skulls and fetishes rattling.

Chapter 14

"Truth is like a rain…"

– Black Elk
from *Black Elk Speaks*

OUTSIDE BY THE ENTRANCE TO THE CAVE, in a manner reminiscent of a ritual, Secret Pipe lit a torch, ignited the kindling, and watched the fire blaze up, consuming the dead owl lying on the scaffold. He said a few words of prayer, then sat, and did not move.

In spite of the many, nagging questions he had, Wolf Rider did not speak. He knew a venerable creature had been lost and a period of mourning was required to pay homage to it. In time, the inquiries came slowly, were asked with respect, and were not done in an intrusive way.

From the Navajo priest, he learned the wicked chief's name was *Ik-tome* and the members of the plundering tribe were called the *Snake People* and were not related to the Hopi, Yuma, Sioux, or any Indian nation the Dine knew of. They were merely a band of heartless people who went around stealing from other tribes, or bartering with individuals eager and not-so-eager to do business with them. The Snake People, Secret Pipe said, were called that because of the many senseless acts of violence and brutality they committed—acts of rape, pillage, and torture against those weaker than themselves. Venom ran through veins, not blood. For obvious reasons, he warned Wolf Rider to stay away from them. When asked where the '*snake village*' was, Secret Pipe would not say exactly. He merely said it was to the west, somewhere in a distant canyon.

"The word you spoke of," said Wolf Rider, "'*Wasichus*,' what does it mean?"

Secret Pipe fell silent, brooding, then got up, and walked inside the cave, refusing to answer.

One Eye returned late that evening and everyone ate what was left of the stew, cold. Throughout the night Wolf Rider wondered more and more about the cave, the Sacred Hole, and his existence. He realized, after spending most of the winter living in such a desolate place, he knew very little about it, knew very little about survival in the canyon, or about Secret Pipe.

Why did the Navajo choose to live alone? Did he not a have a family? A tribe? What purpose did the sand paintings serve? What messages did the other paintings convey? Above all, why were the Snake People so scared of such an innocent-sounding word?

In spite of his persistence, those questions remained unanswered while Wolf Rider fell deeper and deeper into despair. He felt persecuted by his own people, an outcast incapable of having a vision, a man who was powerless to prevent war, powerless to prevent thieves from stealing.

He did not eat, and after several days of not eating, his skin started to stick closer and closer to his ribs. Homesick and undernourished, he was deteriorating physically as well as emotionally day by day.

Late one afternoon, while Secret Pipe was away, Wolf Rider decided there was only one thing left to do. And it required the most drastic commitment of all. To prepare for it, he gathered as much wood as he could. From several animal skins, utilizing a wooden frame, he built a Sweat Lodge outside on the floor of the canyon. He took a pot of water, placed it inside the lodge, arranged a circle of rocks, made a fire within the rocks and sat naked, splashing water against the hot stones, sending plumes of scalding heat and steam up through the smoke hole. At first, he could barely stand it. His skin glistened with sweat, and throughout the rest of the day and following night he remained in the lodge, exposing himself to the heat and steam while silently praying to the gods for forgiveness.

By morning, he was prepared to take his own life.

The only question was—how and by what method. The answer, after spending all night agonizing over it, was simple. The canyon was deep, the facing of the walls often straight down, in some places twice the flight of an arrow. From the top of the canyon, he would plunge feet-first and end it all. There was no turning back once he jumped. One thing remained—how to climb to the top of the canyon.

With no hope of returning home, of seeing Cloud Wing, of seeing his mother and father, or of rejoining his people, his decision was final.

Other than his clothes and knife, he came into this land with few belongings and would leave it that way, lacking in material things. Fully cleansed and more determined that ever, he set out at dawn, searching for a passage to higher ground.

The task was challenging. Time had chipped away at the canyon millennium after millennium, creating cliffs and massive bluffs, plunging at sharp angles. Limestone, sandstone, shale, and rock were layered, more often sheared, cut vertically by erosion, as if a great stonecutter had wielded a giant axe.

He left without saying a word to Secret Pipe. The Navajo had disappeared anyway, again. He had lived alone for many winters and in all probability would adjust to a solitary existence without any problem. Secret Pipe was a survivor. Wolf Rider owed him a great deal and appreciated everything the Dine had done, but somehow it seemed fitting to depart the same way he came. Silently. Unobserved.

* * *

The day was clear, the air cold, tinged with frost.

A bald eagle spread its wings and soared over the canyon walls. It screeched, as if to announce the coming daylight, which now cast a dingy glow across the eastern sky. Wolf Rider headed west, choosing to explore places in the upper canyon he had never seen before. Carrying a walking stick, he followed the dry riverbed, looking for a trail or plateau leading to a ridge above.

After searching all morning, he finally found a formation that appeared to have been created by an avalanche or earthquake. Or by *Ti-ra-wa* himself. Crushed rock and sediment were heaped in a mountainous mass, leading up the southern face of the canyon wall. From where he stood, the slope and texture of the stone, sand, and clay did not seem insurmountable, a difficult climb perhaps, yet promising enough to reach the top. So, with one steady foot at a time, he began his ascent as rocks and stone clattered down the slope below.

Clawing on all fours, he climbed from rock to rock and rim to rim, raising himself from one elevation to another, never in danger of falling or putting himself at risk. His progress was slow but steady, measured sometimes not by height, but by his ability to gain a toehold or purchase where there was none. If it meant going backwards to reach a new level, that is what he did. Several times he looked down, only to realize what little headway he actually had made.

At one point he encountered a nest of rattlesnakes warming themselves in the sun. After tossing a couple of rocks at them, they scattered, hissing, slithering into tiny crevices to hide. Farther up, he found two scorpions nesting in the rocks. He had seen Secret Pipe pinch off their tail and claws and swallow the bodies whole. *How could anything poisonous be good to eat?*—he wondered. Certainly not scorpions or snakes. But hunger was the last thing on his mind. Getting to the top of the canyon was all that mattered.

Oddly enough, there were moments when he was worried about falling to his death by accident. If he died, he wanted it to be his choice. Not fate or a decision made by a god or spirit. In spite of scorpions and snakes and the perilous footing, he had reached a summit, an impasse, the first of two. A ledge of rock rose vertically, not gradually or upon an incline. A cliff. A sheer wall of stone, which he estimated to be about six times his height. Reddish brown sandstone, shale and boulder, hardened by time, towered above him, chunks of it capable of breaking at any second, under the weight of a climber. That was the chance he had to take. And he took it without hesitation.

Gripping a rocky ledge here and there, he steadied himself, making sure neither hand would slip, or a piece of stone would snap or crack. He lifted his body, suspended by the tenuous grip of his fingers, the awkward push of his feet. He was a slow moving spider crawling up the side of a canyon wall, punctuated by crags, crevices, ledges, and slabs of hardened sand, shale, and rock.

It was amazing how tired he grew and how quickly. He had a burning sensation in each of his hands from flexing and grabbing and holding on. All around him, and below, there was the sound of falling rock, of dust pouring, blowing in the wind like rain. Gravel and loose sediment fell. Ledges gave way. Chunks dropped, landing with a loud *crunch*, splitting open layers of fossilized slate. Still, he hung on, sometimes just by his fingertips. From one piece of rock to another he clung, always climbing upward, always higher, never looking down. He reached and clutched again and again, his hands burning, the tendons cramping. He reached one last time and found a flat surface with a hard edge to it. Looking up, all he could see was sky. The summit was an arm's length away. Spent and seemingly incapable of moving another muscle, he strained with all his might, reaching out with his other hand, fingers groping, clawing. A knuckle scraped, the skin tearing against a granite slab. Both hands were bleeding. He pulled. His fist found a bulging rock. His arms were shaking, losing power rapidly. His head rose above the summit, then his neck, chest, stomach, and he lay there, heaving. Winded. About to pass out.

Chapter 15

ACROSS THE BLUFF, with silence stirring and wind-swept air, Wolf Rider walked along the rim of the canyon in search of a ledge. The sun shed its golden light, giving the reddish brown hues of stone a rare and startling clarity. Contrasted against the blueness of the sky, there was no denying the beauty of it all. For someone who started out the morning with grim feelings of despair, it was difficult to consider ending his life on such a glorious day. But now, having climbed to the rim of the summit, he was committed to an act, of which there was no compromise. In his estimation there was one of two ways of doing it— either quick and easy, or, in tribute to *Ti-ra-wa*, honoring the gods and spirits. For a man devoted to the religious practices of the Pawnee, the choice was simple.

Gazing across the bluffs, he could see patches of smoke rising from a distant canyon, perhaps half a day's walk from the gorge. And where there was smoke, there was fire. And where there was fire, there had to be people. But which ones? The Yumas, or those that 'slithered on their bellies?'

Putting aside his curiosity, he made his way to a cliff with a slab of rock extending a few feet out over the precipice, which suited his needs perfectly. From his waistband he removed a pouch and from it he sprinkled dust in all four directions. To the South '*Where the Summer Comes*' and '*All That Gives Power to Grow*'. To the East '*Where the Morning Rises*'…'*Where Light Springs from the Shadow of Night*'. To the North '*Where the Cleansing Wind Blows*'. And finally to the West '*Where the Thunder Beings Live*,' in distant lands '*Where Life is Born*,'— life bearing roots, fins, wings, and feet.

He was reminded of a song a priest once sang while lying at his deathbed: "*…In the dark hours of sleep, death creeps close to the old and young without a sound, without a cry of warning. Spare the young and take the old. Behold me! I am ready to be taken!*"

The irony was not lost on Wolf Rider. Feeling much older than he was, he chanted, "Behold me! I am ready to be taken."

After which, his thoughts gravitated to his mother and father. Swimming in Snake River. Eating gopher tallow. Hunting rabbits with his bow and arrow. Life in *Tuh-parisu* as he once knew it.

Perched precariously, hands reaching upward, he curled the toes of his moccasins over the edge of rock, refusing to look down. One glance from a tall height gave him a feeling of vertigo, so he averted his eyes and allowed his mind to drift as he thought of his first buffalo hunt. Then of Cloud Wing. Riding along with the wind. Holding her in his arms. The graceful gallop of Giant Wolf. The cadence. The sound of plodding hoofs against the rhythm of his heart. And he could imagine that sound now. It seemed to hover at the edge of his perception—a soft steady gait, falling and rising in perfect tempo, clipping across the hardened ground. Yes, he could hear it—the sound of motion. Striding along without effort. Allowing the beast to carry him. He could almost *feel* it. Sense it. It seemed so real.

Then he opened an eye. The sound continued, unabated. Then he opened the other eye and the sound grew louder. Somewhere deep inside of him something was stirring. A breeze was at his back and he wobbled for an instant, almost lost his balance, and glanced down, panicking, feeling his entire life slipping away. The depths of the gorge pulled at him. Swaying, he could feel himself tipping over the edge, plummeting. Yet somehow, impossibly, he remained standing, the worse for it perhaps. A shakiness in his legs came and went with a suddenness. He teetered, righted himself, then pushed at the air for stability. And got it. Just in the nick of time. The soles of his moccasins were now firmly planted on rock. Relieved, he stepped back from the ledge. Breathing deeply, he listened. The sound he heard before was still clip-clopping through the dry riverbed. Once he realized what it was, a surge of excitement whipped through his body. Chills ran up his spine.

The quiet of the canyon had indeed been interrupted by a noise. By hoof beats! Giant Wolf was no mirage, no whim of his imagination.

Spotted brown and white. Long lean muscular legs. It sped along at the urging of its rider—an old man with long gray hair, flowing gently in the wind. The old man guided the beast expertly, clutching its mane. Despite the frenzied pace, the horse, for a moment, held back. Then, with a fire inside it, reared its head and dashed forward, hurling its body like a projectile, gamboling on legs that churned with relentless power. The rider held on, surprised by the sudden burst, slipped, then regained his balance, and drove the animal faster, slapping his hand against its flank, leaning forward, coaxing it, pushing it, insisting that it run at full gallop, giving the impression that both rider and horse were escaping, running from something.

Or *someone.*

Unnoticed until now, the only thing that pursued them was a faithful one-eyed dog, leaping and bounding at the horse's feet.

Whatever intention Wolf Rider had before now became secondary. He cupped his hands to his mouth and yelled, which made the rider look up as the echo rang through the canyon. Once the rider recognized who the caller was, he yelled back, then motioned with his arm, suggesting they meet somewhere along the gorge, as soon as possible.

Frantically, Wolf Rider looked for a passage down. Returning to the place where he made his ascent, he lowered himself by his fingertips and found toeholds in the crevices. With one sure-handed grip at a time, he was able to retrace the way he came. The effort took only half that to climb and half again in terms of duration. Once he reached the canyon floor, Secret Pipe signaled for him to hurry. So Wolf Rider leapt onto the horse's back and off they rode together—followed, of course, by One Eye.

Their meeting, whether decided by the gods or chance, was never discussed, not while they were riding. Wolf Rider never asked why and Secret Pipe made no attempt to explain the urgency of their ride, or how he had found the horse. Upon their arrival at the cave, however, the Dine was besieged with questions. It was only natural for Wolf Rider to wonder where the horse had been. Unfortunately, the inquiries fell on deaf ears. It appeared Secret Pipe had more pressing business to attend to. He asked Wolf Rider to make a fire, then vanished into the tunnel and reappeared a short time later, dragging an object behind him, an object wrapped in a dirty buffalo skin.

Sitting cross-legged by the fire, Wolf Rider remarked, "My Dine friend rides like he was born on Giant Wolf's back."

Secret Pipe did not reply. Instead, he filled a pipe with *chacun sha-sha*, the bark of the red willow. After lighting it, he inhaled deeply as if it were his last puff, and blew out a long stream of smoke. The scent was sweet, almost like wild flowers.

"For too long I have lived alone," Secret Pipe confided. "One day, not long ago, I saw tracks. Tracks of what the Sioux call a *pony*. I had to make a choice. Follow the tracks. Or help a young man I thought was dead. How was I to know the pony was yours."

Pausing, he took another puff. Contentment came to his face and when he spoke again, he voice grew softer. Quieter. "My Pawnee friend showed me he has a strong heart. Almost as strong as *Yiebichai** himself. For a reason I do not know my friend is sad. Among the Dine, we have a word. *Hozho*** it is called. It is the way to happiness, a spirit within each of us *Yiebichai* gives. Although you are not a Dine, perhaps *hozho* can be yours."

"Among the Pawnee," Wolf Rider replied, "we, too, have a word, only it comes from *Ti-ra-wa*. He and the *Nabu'rac* have refused me happiness for the wrongs that I have done." Again, he told him of the war between the Comanches and Pawnees, then related a few incidents that had an impact on his life, including the discovery of an animal he fondly referred to as *Giant Wolf*, his rebellion against the Morning Star Ceremony for the love of Cloud Wing, her mention of the Sacred Hole, a Vision of Light, and his failure in having a vision.

After listening patiently, Secret Pipe narrowed his eyes and said, "The vision you seek may come to you in other ways. I, too, lost my shadow once. I will tell you how. But first I must sing a *Song of Talking God*."

In the language of the Navajo he chanted—

> "*Now I walk with Talking God.*
> *With beauty and goodness in all things*
> *around me I go.*

---

* Grandfather of all Navajo gods; 'Talking God'

** No satisfactory translation; correct thinking in relation to the divine nature of the world

With beauty and goodness, I follow
life forever.
Thus being I, I go."

Staring into the fire, Secret Pipe visualized far away memories.

"It was a long time ago," he said, "before the *Moon When Ponies Shed* (May). Until then I had never heard of the *Wasichus*. When I left the Bella Coola, I was no longer a slave.

"Traveling *Where-the-Sun-Rises*, I wandered far, far through the Land of the Smokey Earth, across rivers and lakes until I came to a place called the Black Hills, and there I met up with a party of Lakota Sioux. The Sioux had many ponies, which I had never seen before. And for many winters I lived with the Sioux, hunted buffalo, and took care of their ponies. And that is how I learned to speak Lakota Sioux.

"While we were out hunting one day, I heard stories of a strange new people, what they called the *Wasichus*, people who came from a land far, far away, beyond the desert and mountains. From what I heard of the *Wasichus* I did not like. The Sioux said there were so many of them, you could not count them all. They were like grains of sand in the desert. According to the chief, even the Apaches, the fiercest warriors of all, were afraid of the *Wasichus*. Myself, I was afraid of no one. I had survived attacks by Crow, Cheyenne, Blackfeet…wolves, *taraha*, Monster Fish. If I was going to die, I believed it would be by the hand of *Yiebichai*."

He mentioned the years he spent with the Sioux, how he roamed the Great Plains, hunting *taraha*. It was a period of time, he said, filled with adversity when he was told tales of the *Wasichus*, of lands being invaded by vicious men, of killings, mutilation, sickness, atrocities inflicted upon the Indian. Eventually, he left the Sioux to return to his people, having never seen the *Wasichus* himself, and from there he described an idyllic life, one where he was reunited with his mother, sisters, and cousins…was married, became a father, a priest, an *hataali*, a Maker of Medicine, and eventually lived a peaceful existence, caring for his family.

"The Dine were happy," he said, "at war with no one. Meat was plentiful, the maize thick and tall. *Hozho* had come to everyone. *Yiebichai* was kind to us all.

"Then one day a Dine priest returned to his village after a long prayer march to tell the people of strange new *beasts* he had seen. He said they were *Standing Bears* who wore stone shirts, rode upon *Giant Wolves*, and pulled tepees on round legs made from trees. Though this person who said this was an *hataali*, he was also very young. The Dine laughed at him because they did not believe his story.

"They gave him the name of *Bear Crier*. He did not like this name or the laughter, so to stop the Dine from laughing, he left the village one day to capture a Standing Bear. By the banks of the Crooked River he found one searching for yellow stones in the shallow waters and brought him home to prove that he was telling the truth. But the Standing Bear was a man whose hair was white and skin was pale, as if it had never touched the sun. The *Pale Skin*, as the Dine now called the Standing Bear, had ugly hair all over his face and spoke a tongue no one had heard before.

"We kept him for a while, listening to the strange way he talked, watching even the stranger way he behaved, and were about to let him go when more Pale Skins, on an angry wind, attacked the Dine. The Pale Skins fought with strange, powerful weapons. *Storm Sticks!* Their storm sticks spoke thunder, shot lightning, and killed many frightened Dine in a hurry! But our arrows could not pierce their stone shirts.

"The wife and daughter of Bear Crier died from stabs of the Pale Skin's lightning. Bear Crier mourned their deaths…blamed himself for the raiding of his village. He became, as you say, a *shadowless man*. Unworthy fool that he was, he abandoned the Dine and wandered far to finish out a small, small life. But when he reached a peaceful place, said to be the Beginning of Earth, he renamed himself, hoping to become a man again, hoping to find *hozho*.

"After many winters, he sought forgiveness from *Yiebichai* and the Spirits of the Other World by being their servant. And by being their servant he escaped the Pale Skins, what the Sioux call *Wasichus*."

Secret Pipe turned from the fire to look at Wolf Rider. "I have told you this for a reason. Today I went to uncover something Bear Crier buried a long time ago. It is here, under the cloak." He unwrapped the bundle beside him. Inside was a bronze Spanish breastplate. "Here. I give you the stone shirt. This, and the story of my paintings, should replace your Vision of Light. Return home. Make peace with the Comanches. Those who are wise will understand and forgive. No one understands better than Bear Crier that war is no good. Remember this. A strong man, a good man, a wise and clever man, one who is swift afoot who can see all—he is a man who will one day be chief."

Pausing, he took another puff from the pipe. "And here is a gift for the Comanche woman." From the bundle he produced a necklace of panther teeth and handed it to Wolf Rider. "Tell her it is a gift. The only teeth an old man can give." And with that, he smiled, exposing what few teeth he had.

Wolf Rider could not help but smile back. His eyes passed from the stone shirt to the necklace. Finally, he reached down and offered his only possession. "Let the hand that was once Bear Crier's take this Pawnee knife. And when you use it, think of me."

And for a moment, just a moment, there was a feeling of peace between them as they smoked *chacun sha-sha*, the bark of the red willow.

Chapter 16

"Pawnee, you must go! Wake up! Hurry! You must go!"

Wolf Rider opened an eye. Secret Pipe was leaning over him, shaking him. The dog was growling, standing by the entrance of the cave, tail pointed, rigid—a sign that something was wrong. Beyond, barely visible in the firelight, Giant Wolf was already packed with provisions, buffalo sacks containing food and water.

Wolf Rider rubbed the sleep from his eyes. Sitting up, he was helped to his feet. For all he knew, he was still dreaming. Dazed and confused, he looked around. Secret Pipe was now kicking sand over the fire, trying to smother it. When that didn't seem to work, he grabbed a pot of water and poured the contents over the flames, dousing them completely. The fire sizzled—embers hissing, a voluminous cloud of smoke and steam shooting upward as the cave suddenly turned pitch black.

Everything was cloaked in black, shadow against shadow, swathed in a sort of nebulous haze, like a miasma lingering over a swamp. Outside, it was cold and damp, the ground blanketed with a fine powder of frost.

As his eyes adjusted to the darkness, he could see pale streaks of light forming across the base of the canyon. Rocks, cliffs, bluffs, sky. Everything was caught in transition—from the obscurity of night to the early stages of dawn.

At the front of the cave, he heard Secret Pipe say, "Follow the dry river toward the *Rise of the Sun*! And remember! The Bright Star, the North Star! Keep it here…"—he pointed at left shoulder—"at your side when you travel at night."

Without further delay, Wolf Rider was led outside. He hesitated when a rock fell, clattering and tumbling across the canyon floor. Both men turned, staring anxiously at the gorge.

"Quickly! Go!" Secret Pipe cried. "The Snake People are coming!"

The dog retreated, barking, the hair along the back of its neck standing straight up.

Wolf Rider froze. It came to him suddenly. The thought of Giant Wolf's return flashed through his mind like a bolt of lightning. It was perfectly clear how the mystery unfolded. He briefly pictured an old man sneaking through the village at night...

The only sounds he could hear were the Snake People snoring. Past tepees, campfires, and sleeping dogs he crept, hunched over, tip-toeing through the darkness. The horse whinnied nervously. Someone woke up, saw him, and yelled. Pretty soon everyone was running around, yelling, thinking they were being attacked. Warriors grabbed their bows, their war clubs, and tomahawks. Through the pandemonium the old man rode, slapping...driving the animal beneath him, urging it on. Unfaltering, Giant Wolf found its stride. With amazing sure-footedness it galloped, tail streaming, legs churning, the sleek elegance of its magnificence reflected in its power and speed. The people were left gawking, as if they'd seen a ghost, while the chief gnashed his teeth and swore vengeance upon the thief, a man so foolish, so reckless as to risk his own life.

The audacity of it! The boldness!

It was almost laughable.

"*Hee-ya! Hee-ya!*" Secret Pipe whispered harshly.

Blinking, Wolf Rider came out of his trance and was given a bow, a quiver of arrows, and finally the stone shirt. Each was thrust at him, not handed. He stared at the Spanish breastplate, reluctant to take it.

"Hurry! You must leave!" Secret Pipe cried. Bending stiffly at the waist, he picked up the dog and held its mouth closed to keep it from barking.

At the same time, Giant Wolf whinnied and tossed its head up and down, growing highly agitated. Wolf Rider managed to slip the stone shirt over his chest and pull the quiver over his shoulder. Clutching the rope tied to the animal's neck, he grabbed its mane and jumped on.

Another rock fell, this time closer.

An instant later, Giant Wolf lurched and shuffled its feet nervously. Wolf Rider had to yank on the rope to steady it. He glanced to his left and back, and without seeing or hearing anything could tell the horse was about to bolt at any moment.

"Where will you go?" he asked Secret Pipe. "What will you do?"

Secret Pipe said nothing. Instead, he slapped the rear of the horse and watched it lunge forward. As he waved, he said—

"Peace! That is how you will find your shadow, my friend. I will ask *Yeibichai* to watch over you."

With a click of its hoofs, Giant Wolf galloped off, and Secret Pipe whispered—

> *"Now he runs with Talking God.*
> *With beauty and goodness in all things*
> *around him, he goes.*
> *With beauty and goodness, he follows*
> *life forever.*
> *As he rides, he goes—*
> *a man of peace."*

Silently, Secret Pipe withdrew into the shadows of the cave, hugging One Eye firmly in his arms. Near the entrance, he heard the flight of an arrow, then another, then another, followed by war cries and footsteps—coming closer and closer.

He crept away as quietly as he could, retreating into the tunnel, then into the cavern buried deep in the bedrock where he was certain no one would find him.

Outside in the canyon, beyond the range of arrows, Wolf Rider halted Giant Wolf and glanced over his shoulder. In the gradual daylight he could barely make out the dark figures as they converged on the cave. One of them stood out more than the others, a man wearing a long feathered headdress and pale ermine coat—

Ik-tome.

Wolf Rider raised up on his mount, holding his bow high, and shouted, "*Hoy-ahhh!*"

The two exchanged stares.

Then, with a tug on the mane, Wolf Rider made his way up the gently curving slope of the canyon, the first rays of sunlight shining off his gold Spanish breastplate.

Eastward he rode, across a *Land of Rock, Cliff, and Stone*, toward the mountains.

Toward *Tuh-parisu.*

BOOK FIVE: PEACEMAKER
Long Journey Home

Chapter 17

A WESTERN WIND, RAW AND BRISK, RATTLED THE PINES.

It was now *Moon of the Waking Bear** and the cold mountain air was still wreathed in frost, the High Country coated in white. Spring thaw was approaching and throughout the brooks and streams ice was melting, riverbanks were overflowing with water. Animal tracks dotted the snow-covered ground as the deer, the fox, and rabbit emerged from their hideaways in preparation for the coming season.

The Pawnees had not been dutiful, but the reason was not for lack of concern. They had fought three consecutive battles against the Comanches. Each had sustained substantial losses and still there was no treaty. Compounding this, another vicious enemy had spread throughout the Pawnee camp: an outbreak of disease. A few fires burned. Lodges were left unbuilt while tepees housed the sick. Sentries slumped at their posts. Dogs ran around, neglected. Women straggled about, dispensing food, keeping the fires lit, the sick snuggled in furs and blankets. Medicine men, hooded in grotesque *curing* masks, hobbled about the camp, shaking their medicine rattles, making charms, and wailing with desperate and ceaseless song, trying to expel the sickness from those stricken.

In words quiet and low, priests of the Evening Star and Morning Star and those of the *Hedushka* prayed to *Ti-ra-wa*, "Father, you are the Healer. Your children are miserable and cold. Tell us what to do to make us strong…"

Day after day, huddled around a campfire, the priests, chief, war chief, and members of Council kept their eyes fixed on the slopes of the

---

* February – March

surrounding mountains, watching for Comanche war parties. Comanche scouts had been spying on the village since the first battle, waiting like vultures to prey on the weak and the dying. Twice during the night Comanches had crept into camp to steal a few horses, but each attempt was thwarted. Between the foiled theft of horses, an occasional attack and constant spying, there was little rest for the Pawnees. And with each passing incident, there were more and more discussions about leaving the mountains and returning to the prairie.

As was customary, a pipe was passed among the leaders. As each man drew a puff, he would bow his head and say, "Earth, to you I smoke," then after another puff, would lift his head and say, "Sky, to you I smoke," and, finally, after several more puffs, would acknowledge the spirits of the Four Winds and speak what was on his mind.

"For many winters," one warrior said, "we lived where the grass was tall. Now since the *Moon of the Dying Grass* (October) we have lived among the Shiny Mountains and have known nothing but war and misery. Two days ago, riders returned to tell us rain and snow have fallen on our homeland. They say they saw so many buffalo they could not count them all. Grass was trampled bare by bulls running side by side. Here we grow hungry. And the Comanches watch us day and night. My brothers, I ask you. Is this what you want? To live in a place where there are no buffalo? A place where the enemy hides, waiting to attack?"

A loud chorus of *no's* resounded.

"Do you not miss the taste of buffalo meat? Living where our fathers and grandfathers lived?"

"*Aye! Aye!*" they replied.

Next to him, another warrior said, "What Little Bear says is true. No one misses the Land of Buffalo more than me. But my wife and daughters are sick, too weak to travel. Many of you have family who cannot walk. Who will carry them home?"

Back and forth they bickered and debated when, all at once, several men stood up and stared at a distant clearing.

"Look!" a warrior cried. "The son of Two Buffalo!"

Stunned, the Morning Star priest rose to his feet. "Thief! Lover of Comanches!"

The camp, despite all the sickness and inactivity, suddenly came alive. Dogs growled and barked as if set upon by vicious animals.

People rushed from their tepees, carrying tomahawks, knives, one form of weapon or another, yelling, "*Charik waik-ta!** *Charik waik-ta!*" certain they were coming under siege by a Comanche war party. Only in the confusion did they realize a 'call to arms' was unnecessary. Never before had one person riled so many without provocation or threat of violence. In ever increasing numbers, those who could stand and walk, who had the strength to drag their feet through the wet snow, gathered at the edge of camp while the chief, along with a priest and two others, proceeded into the clearing.

At the base of the valley, past a thicket of pines, a young man clothed in trappings of fur led his mount. He slowed it to a trot, then to a walk as he entered a ravine and crossed to the other side.

The horse, for all its grace and splendor, showed the effects of much travel. Its winter coat was ragged, its body lean. Breathing hard, it held its head low, and although its gait was a mere walk, it appeared to labor under the weight of the travois.

The rider, however, did not look tired at all. He seemed relaxed, at ease with himself. He rode with pride, with dignity, back straight, shoulders arched high. Once he crossed the ravine, the dogs stopped barking, as if they could sense something in him, a familiarity, a calmness, that he posed no threat, no harm to anyone.

In the middle of a snow-covered clearing the two sides met. They stood face to face, the son of Two Buffalo filled with expectations and longings for his family, and the four who opposed him, resentful of an act he committed a long time ago.

"Why have you come back?" the chief shouted.

Wolf Rider did not reply. He looked at the crowd and recognized relatives and old friends alike—

Night Scout, a young warrior. Six Kill, the village Crier. His half brother, Raven Chief. Rattling Hawk. Rainmaker, slayer of buffalo. Kicking Bear, Whirlwind Chaser—both members of the *Hedushka*. His childhood companion, Little Wolf Boy. A fearless hunter named Rising Smoke. Dozens of others with whom he once shared food and laughter.

Of the four men standing before him, two had no bearing on his life whatsoever. There were two, however, who did—

---

* a war cry—"*the enemy is upon us!*"

Red Thunder. Chief of the *Wolf Pa'ni*. His chief.

Cornplanter. Priest of the Morning Star Ceremony. His enemy.

"Where are my mother and father?" Wolf Rider asked.

The crowd remained quiet. From Rattling Hawk to Little Wolf Boy, he was looked upon with indifference, as a stranger, their faces cold, expressionless.

They saw someone much older and different than the boy who called himself Flying Fox. Flying Fox was shy, at times introverted, a dreamer, a boy who preferred to be alone, who respected the customs of the tribe and never challenged authority or made trouble in any way.

Wolf Rider, on the other hand, appeared bigger, stronger, and evoked a confidence that, as a child, he lacked. Perhaps the most telling change of all had to do with his hair. He defied tradition by not wearing a scalp lock, the *pariki*, Horn of the Bull, a long ribbon of hair that ran down the middle of the skull. He wore his hair full and long.

"Why have you come back?" the chief repeated. "We have illness. We have war. Cornplanter says you have brought both upon us."

Wolf Rider ignored the question. "I want to see my mother and father."

There was a slow turning of heads, whispers, too quiet to hear.

"Your mother is sick," Red Thunder replied. "No one can see her."

"And my father?"

"Gone! In the mountains, hunting," shouted Cornplanter. "No one welcomes you here!"

Red Thunder took two steps forward, raised his lance, and pounded it into the frozen ground. "It is a bad time for us. The corn is gone. The meat, scarce. And the White Tails have scattered." He waved his hand dismissively, then gestured to the surrounding mountains. "The enemy lies waiting like vultures. Our lodges are filled with the weak and the dying. There is no food. Our nation's hoop has been broken." He made a gesture with his lance—of snapping it across his knee. "And it is because of you. You!"

There were rumblings of dissatisfaction from the crowd, a feeling of resentment toward Wolf Rider, as if he were to blame for it all.

Red Thunder motioned for quiet, "In the morning, the Council will sit and talk. We will decide what to do with you. Until then, you are not wanted here."

"Leave!" Cornplanter shouted. "Go sleep with the Comanches! It is with them you have made your bed!"

Wolf Rider tried to hide his disappointment. He had come so far. Had been through so much. Just moments before his heart leapt with joy at seeing the camp. Now he felt as if he had no home, no people, and no place to go.

Worst of all, he had to sleep another night in the cold.

He knew earning his way back into the tribe would not come easy. No amount of talk would convince anyone of that. Acceptance had to be achieved by deed or action. Nothing else. And to do that he needed a plan, a strategy that would bring an end to the war and place him back in the good graces of his people.

Without another word, he nodded to Red Thunder, then to the others.

Slowly, he pulled the reins to the side and urged Giant Wolf into a trot. Together horse and rider wandered through the clearing, across the ravine, and disappeared into the trees.

Chapter 18

*"...On the path of peace
our nation shall walk..."*

Dusk was lengthening the shadows, drawing down a frigid mass of air.

Wolf Rider made camp below a ridge, overlooking the valley where new *Tuh-parisu* lay. Quickly, he realized he was losing the battle with the cold. By the time it took him to feed the horse, bind its feet so it would not run away, then clear a patch of snow where he could lie down, his hands had grown numb, nearly frost bitten. During the day, the surface of the snow had melted. A crusty layer of ice had formed which crunched when he walked upon it. As he moved, his feet sank into the wet slush beneath, causing water to soak into his moccasins, leaving the flesh half frozen.

As the evening wore on, he knew the weather would turn, the snow would harden, and the air would grow bitter cold. It was a bit frightening— to think the worst was yet to come.

It wasn't that he neglected to prepare for the weather. He did. Throughout his journey he had killed scores and scores of rabbits, which provided enough pelts, along with the skin of the otter, beaver, and wolf, to make a variety of clothing to protect against the elements—a fur-lined turban headdress, coat, leggings, moccasins, plus a heavy, fur-lined blanket for Giant Wolf, and two thick, bedcovers for himself. In doing so he had become a skilled hunter, skinner, and tracker.

The stone shirt was too awkward to sleep in, so he removed it, threw on his coat of rabbitskin, spread a cover of pelts on the ground, then wrapped another lengthwise around his body, and tried to make himself as comfortable as possible. In spite of this, he was still shivering. His biggest fear, of course, was that he would freeze, so he decided to make a fire. Try as he would, his hands couldn't grab. His fingers couldn't squeeze. Both were incapable of holding much of anything. He had no sensation in his feet, only a biting numbness brought on by the cold. He thrashed about, stamped his feet, and threshed his hands against his sides in order to restore the feeling. When sufficiently revived, he went to work.

From the trees he collected pieces of loose timber and set them near a fallen log. After scraping the bark off the log, he piled a handful of pine needles over a bare spot and placed a stick vertically over it. Rubbing the stick very fast between his palms, the stick bore into the trunk, causing friction, then fire to the needles, over which he heaped more wood. Slowly, as the flames spread, he gazed at the small, expanding light and said—

"Fire, captured from *Him-Who-Watches-Bright*. Capture the memory of her, the Comanche woman, who has stolen my heart. Give me warmth, will you, Fire? Do not let me grow cold."

Almost every night throughout the winter, from *Moon-of-the-Popping-Tree* (December) to *Moon-of-the-Dark-Red-Calf* (February), he had built a fire. Rarely did he lack wood to burn. Yet there were occasions where he didn't want to bring attention to himself—when a party of Arapahos camped nearby, or tracks belonging to a Shoshone hunting party posed a threat.

Oftentimes, he slept in places where no man should sleep—on a bed of stone, a grassy knoll where rattlesnakes nested, a frozen stretch of ground, or in a forest where black bears prowled—always where peril existed.

Each time he knew the risks he was taking.

Now he realized he was taking the biggest risk of all. He had seen several tracks, not of animals, but of men wearing moccasins, wandering up and down the mountain trails. There was no way of telling if they were friendly or not. The tracks were old, soft around the edges where the snow had melted. And from the deep claw marks in the snow, he knew all too well that bears were coming out of their hibernation with voracious appetites and an insatiable desire to hunt and kill. Of course, wolves were no different, less likely to stalk man as a source of food perhaps, but, having survived the winter with little or next to nothing to eat, they were on the trail for meat—of any kind. Man, animal, fish—they made no distinction. Their ability to make a kill, while putting themselves in as little danger as possible, was the only thing that mattered. The scarcity of food drove them into a frenzy. At no other time during any other season—spring, summer, or fall—were they so crazed, so driven as make them unpredictable, more aggressive in their lust for food.

Necessary as a fire was to keep the animals at bay, its light could be seen far across the valley which acted as both a comfort and source of concern. After all, who would see it?

Wolf Pa'ni? Or Comanche?

Once the fire was made, he sat beside it, warming his hands and feet. The smoke reminded him of venison, slowly roasting over a campfire. He could almost hear the fat melting, taste the juices mingling with the tender meat.

How hungry he was—

And lonely.

During his travels, the worst thing of all was having no one to talk to. Being by himself for days on end made him think crazy thoughts. Sometimes he had conversations with himself just to break the silence, or he would talk to Giant Wolf, speak to it as he would a friend—about anything, about life in general, or a particular concern at the moment. Is this the trail home, my friend? Are you hungry? What is the Comanche woman doing? Does she think of me, this woman who calls herself Cloud Wing?

Absently, his mind wandered, as did his eyes.

Shimmering in the firelight, he noticed the Spanish breastplate lying at his feet and wondered what his father would make of it if he were sitting here. As he had done many times when alone on the trail, he pretended…

Appearing somewhere in the dark imaginings of smoke, he watched as Two Buffalo unrolled shanks of roasted meat from a calfskin and passed one of them to his son. They ate ravenously, gnawing them down the bone.

"*Ah*, what is this?" said Two Buffalo. He leaned over, picked up the breastplate, and ran his hands over the surface.

Wolf Rider could feel himself grinning. "A *stone shirt*," he replied.

"*Mmmm*—strong. Where did you find it?"

"An old man gave it to me."

"Old man?"

"Yes. He calls himself a Dine. He taught me many things."

"So, this old man, what did he teach you?"

"How to be clever. Like a fox."

Wolf Rider smiled and took another bite of meat. He could actually taste the delicacy of its flavor, smell the aroma of seared fat...the sweet bitterness of a slight char. Having Two Buffalo near, even though it was make-believe, was reassuring. Together they sat, chewing quietly, listening to the sounds of the night.

Snow fell from a ridge above, crashing with a heavy thud.

A slight breeze shook the pines.

Wings flapped. There was a sudden pounce of a body as it landed on the ground. A night owl hooted, snatched its prey, and flew away.

Across the valley, in the hollows of a distant forest, an animal was silenced as it was being attacked. It began and ended abruptly as it always did. A cry of terror. Followed by a brief whimper.

It was a the way of the *Nabu'rac*—the way it had always been, which reminded Wolf Rider just how perilous his situation had become.

Even with his father beside him, there was a certain desperation in all of this. He could feel it.

Wolf Rider was, after all, a solitary man, in exile, famished, thirsting, vulnerable to the elements. If he was clever like a fox, he would do something about it.

But what?

One thing came to mind, a prayer he once heard his father say. He remembered only a portion of it. After a party of Cheyennes had been defeated in battle, Two Buffalo was asked what he hoped the future would bring.

Wolf Rider repeated the words: "On the path of peace our nation shall walk."

Two Buffalo looked up, surprised. "Peace? What is this peace you speak of?"

"In your hands lies a secret, father. Magic! Soon I will make peace with the Comanches."

"The Comanches will not make peace."

"I know of one who will. And some day I will marry her."

"I am afraid you have slept alone too many nights, my son. No marriage will make a treaty."

"It will, if the Comanches do not kill me first."

Chewing reflectively on a piece of meat, Two Buffalo grinned and replied, "Good."

And like a dream, the image of Two Buffalo faded, drifting away with the wistful clouds of smoke.

An idea, however, lingered.

Quietly, Wolf Rider crawled inside the bed of rabbitskins and watched the fire flicker and smolder.

The first thing he had to do, he realized, was find the Comanche village. Since his own people had banished him from theirs, he knew he could not depend on anyone else for help.

In honor of his father, he vowed in the morning, at the dawning of the Daybreak Star, to begin the search.

* * *

Accustomed as he was to traveling alone, he slept lightly, aware of the slightest sound, with Giant Wolf always near to warn of danger. For the better part of a year, from *Moon-When-the-Cherries-are-ripe* (July) to *Moon-of-the-Waking-Bear* (February-March), Wolf Rider had experienced more than most men twice his age. He had survived famine, drought, prairie fire, a sand storm, an attack from a panther, a black bear, insects, Comanches, roaming far and wide under conditions the most trail-hardened hunter had seldom seen. Not once, but twice he had attempted a vision quest, and throughout that time he had faced adversity in places familiar and foreign to him—desert, mountains, canyons, and High Plains—while subjecting himself to torture for the sake of *Ti-ra-wa,* the *Nabu'rac,* his tribe, and family.

There was not an animal he had not hunted, a skill he had not honed, or situation within reason he did not feel capable of overcoming. If he learned nothing else, it was during these odysseys that he felt more alive than at any other time, and that survival rested in those experiences.

As he was about to doze off, he heard a soft rustling of tree limbs, a snap, and, the most disturbing of all, a steady crackling of snow.

Giant Wolf stirred.

Wolf Rider waited, listening, and reached for his knife.

Once on a cold night many moons ago, he noticed the glow of eyes reflecting off the campfire and was able to distinguish—by smell, intuition, or some developed sense—a wolf from a coyote, solely on the basis of their eyes. Another time, during his return home, recognizing again by smell or innate ability, he avoided an attack from an angry moose because he sensed it. Whether he sensed its anger or heard the scuffling of its hoofs, he did not know. The point is, *he knew*. Just as he knew the countless times when the hazards of the trail presented themselves.

Such as now—

Resting his ear to the ground, he listened for footsteps. The camp was quiet. The wind calm. A sudden stillness had settled throughout the clearing. Instinctively, he could tell someone was watching from the trees.

Moments later, he heard a crunching of snow to his left.

Someone was running.

Wolf Rider threw his bed cover aside and jumped to his feet. Off he chased—down a blind path, through patches of scrub and dormant brush. The intruder, meanwhile, had sprinted past a stand of trees, as if he could see perfectly in the darkness. Unfortunately for Wolf Rider, he was not as sure or as swift. He tore his leggings running through a thicket and stopped. There was silence all around him—silence in the trees to his left, to his right, those in front, and those in back. The cold mountain air hung without a whisper. Moonlight trickled through the treetops, spilling shadowy images of branches and tree trunks throughout the nightshade.

One of the shadows moved.

"Do not run, Pawnee!" warned a voice. "Snake Boy has an arrow aimed at your back."

Wolf Rider knew at once it was a Comanche. As soon as he heard the name he was reminded of the Snake People and thoughts of evil and malicious things raced through his head.

"How do you know I am a Pawnee?" Wolf Rider asked. "I am not sick like the others. My hair is long."

"Your hair is long because you have not cut it," said Snake Boy. "And you are not sick only because you have not lived with your people."

"How do you know this?"

"I know…because you are Wolf Rider, the one who gave my sister the bear skin."

Snake Boy stepped into the moonlight, revealing himself. He wore a thick winter coat, was stocky, about as tall as Wolf Rider, had dark lanky hair hanging to his shoulders, broad cheekbones covered in war paint. And the bow he held was flexed, nocked with an arrow.

As he turned to leave, Wolf Rider tried to anticipate when to make his escape. He had no idea a party of Comanches was waiting in the clearing ahead. By the time he saw them, it was too late. As one of the warriors reached out to touch the horse, Snake Boy shouted—

"No! The Giant Wolf is mine! Here is the Pawnee you said cannot be taken. I have taken him. See!"

Wolf Rider saw the stone shirt lying on the ground and bent over to pick it up.

"Leave it!" shouted Snake Boy.

A second warrior pushed Wolf Rider aside, reached down, and grabbed the stone shirt in both hands. He eyed the thing from top to bottom, shook it, turned it upside down, grunted, then rubbed his hands across the back and front, puzzled by the size, weight, and shape of it. After further inspection, making odd little noises of dissatisfaction, he shrugged and threw the breastplate aside.

Wolf Rider watched it roll into the bushes. And with it his plan rolled into obscurity.

Chapter 19

THE SUN WAS JUST RISING OVER THE PEAKS of the snow-covered mountains. In the valley below, the Comanche village sat—on an open, flat strip of land between converging streams, curls of smoke rising from the tepees.

From a bluff to the northeast, a sentry's smoke signal announced the approach of a small party. An alert was given and several members of the tribe flocked to the edge of the camp. Murmurs of surprise swept through the gathering when they saw Snake Boy and six Comanche warriors leading a strange and magnificent animal by a rope. Behind it staggered a young man whose hands were tied at the wrists and feet were loosely bound at the ankles, limiting their movement.

As the arriving party drew closer, Snake Boy shouted, "I have captured a giant wolf…and the feared Pawnee!"

A loud cheer went up, followed by war cries, whoops, and a pounding of drums.

At the rear of the procession Wolf Rider carried himself with as much dignity as he could. He trailed the horse into the water, through a shallow rapids, stepping from stone to stone up and over the bank into the awaiting crowd.

Most of the attention, however, was fixed not on him, but upon the remarkable spotted animal that stood on four legs and towered above him. Reaction ranged from curious and shy, to a peculiar kind of reverence, almost as if it were a god or spirit wrapped in the skin of a mythological beast. Some viewed it as a '*short-haired wolf*,' a strange '*breed of buffalo*,' an '*antelope without horns*,' a '*long-legged stag*.'

Hands reached out to touch it, to see if it were real or not, raking their fingers across its shaggy winter coat, stroking its mane, patting its sides, captivated by an animal most of them had never seen before.

Amused by it all, Snake Boy grabbed a hold of the prisoner's rope, tugged it violently with one hand, and shoved him to the ground with the other.

"This…" he said, gesturing to the horse, "is the Great Wolf that runs like the wind. And here…"—he picked up a handful of snow and flung it at Wolf Rider—"is the Pawnee dog, the one they say cannot be killed."

All eyes turned from the horse to the prisoner.

"Pawnee! Pawnee!" they shouted.

Children poked him with sticks, slashed imaginary tomahawks at his sides, shoulders, and back, then brazenly counted coup—*tat-i-ki*—while screaming and yelling and raising their voices in a *tremolo* of frenzy.

"The Pawnee surrendered without a fight!" Snake Boy cried. "Look! He is weak like all the others! Death to the *pi-ta'-da*!*"

"Death to the *pi-ta'-da*!" the crowd chanted.

In disgrace and ridicule, Wolf Rider was taken to a ceremonial pole at the far end of the village and tied to it by his hands and feet.

Throughout the remainder of the day, tribal leaders sat in a tepee where the rumblings of war echoed like distant claps of thunder, where the capture of a horse inspired them and that of a *pi-ta'-da* only served to embolden all the more.

The meeting of the Council ended before dusk and it was decided there would be a feast promoting Snake Boy to the level of his elders.

"A celebration for the coming age of Snake Man!" proclaimed the chief. "I, Quanah, speak not as a father, but as Chief of the Red River. A boy he is no more!"

Soon preparations were made for the feast. Women hung pots from poles and slabs of meat over fire pits. In the pots they poured water, corn, and lots and lots of fish, which quickly simmered, steaming up the air with the savory smell of *succotash*. For the occasion, everyone wore their finest leggings, coats, and dresses of embroidered buckskin, each elaborately decorated with sashes, beads, and braided deer tails. At nightfall, they huddled around the campfires, eating and singing, accompanied by flutes, rattles, and drums. Spirits rose with such passion

---

* Comanche word for *enemy*

the earth seemed to vibrate, the moon to melt behind a rhythmic flow of clouds. Snake Man relished the attention given him by all.

During the festivities, the chief led Giant Wolf into camp. He walked with pride, head flung back, hand on his hip, leading the animal around for everyone to see.

"Here," said Quanah as he stopped to face his son, "The Giant Wolf is yours. Now you may count Pawnee coup."

The people gave their approval by raising their voices like a great howling wind. Fires glowed on excited faces as Snake Man paraded his property around the circle of admirers. The wind blew. And sparks flew upward into the sky like shooting stars as everyone hollered—

"Ride him!"—"Run him!"—"Show us, Snake Man!"

In a rash display of arrogance, Snake Man proceeded to mount the horse.He jumped. His belly landed on the curve of its spine. Giant Wolf spun. And he found himself being tossed to the ground, sprawled on his back. Dazed, he shook his head while the amused crowd snickered and laughed and cheered him on again. This time he mounted from the opposite side. He lifted a leg, stretched, and hopped with the other foot, but neglected to take up the reins. As the animal galloped away, he bounced into the air and again, with arms and legs flailing, fell awk-wardly to the ground.

And again everyone laughed.

Angry and embarrassed, Snake Man dusted himself off.

Before he could try to mount it a third time, there was a distant cry, that of a bird calling—"*Ka-coo! Ka-coo!*" The revelers were so taken by fits of convulsive laughter no one heard it. Giant Wolf, however, did. It was a sound it was intimately familiar. Its ears perked up. It whinnied. It pawed at the ground and, with tail streaming, trotted to the far end of camp where it nudged Wolf Rider with its snout. For the first time that evening the Pawnee was not ignored.

All at once the snickering stopped. Everyone grew quiet.

The chief stood up and rushed toward the prisoner with strides long and swift, as if intending to do harm. Half of the revelers were at his heels. The rest remained behind, muttering to themselves as they wondered what Quanah was about to do when all at once Snake Man, in a fit of jealousy, pushed past the throng of onlookers, shoved Giant Wolf aside, and grabbed the prisoner by the throat.

"How do you wish to die? A knife? Spear? Should I cut you up and feed the pieces to the dogs?"

"No!" shouted Quanah. "There is no honor in killing a man who cannot defend himself."

Snake Man released his hands and stood back, allowing Wolf Rider to catch his breath. With little to lose, while still gasping for air, Wold Rider seized the moment to ask, "May I speak?"

The chief turned, eyes blazing. "If you speak, *pi-ta'-da*, I will choke you myself!"

"Let him speak!" demanded Cloud Wing as she made her way through the crowd. "This is the Pawnee who saved my life. Let him speak!" And with an expression both uncompromising and compassionate, she turned her back to Wolf Rider, folded her arms in an act of defiance, and faced the one man who had the power to decide the fate of the *pi-ta'-da*.

In spite of his authority, Quanah was at a loss of what to do. He looked at his daughter and then at his son. After consulting with another chief for a moment, he appeared to make up his mind. Gripping the handle of his knife, he cautioned the prisoner, "Be quick, Pawnee. Say what you must. But there will be trouble for you and your people if you deceive me."

Wolf Rider could feel everyone staring at him. One misspoken word, a lie, anything that could be taken in a negative way, and he knew he was as good as dead.

"You talked of the ways of honor," he said. "Among the Pawnee, we have honor, too."

"The honor of dogs!" declared Snake Man.

"The honor I speak of is something we all seek. Peace! I have come to make a treaty."

Everyone began shouting at once.

Wolf Rider hollered, "Too many have died. Why are we at war? No Pawnee has ever attacked a Comanche." Again he was shouted down. Undeterred, he persisted, "I come to you not just with words, but to make a challenge…"

"Do not listen to him!" cried Snake Man. "He is a coward. He is full of tricks."

"You would make a challenge…against us?" said the chief.

"Cut these ropes. And I will prove that I am a man of peace."

Quanah slid his knife from the sheath. "And who is it you wish to challenge. Me? My son?"

"Anyone. As long as he can shoot an arrow."

"I warned you," said Quanah, clenching his teeth. "I have ways of making it so you cannot speak." And with one quick motion of his hand, he mimicked the cutting out of a tongue.

Wolf Rider did not flinch, cower, or react in any way. Instead he said, calmly, "The challenge I make to you is this. If you let me go, after one day Giant Wolf and I will return. Choose your best hunter, a man with a good eye…a firm hand. He stands forty paces away. And strikes me with an arrow…here…" He lowered his head, indicating a spot on his chest. "At forty paces, even your son cannot miss."

"Let me shoot the arrow now," said Snake Man.

"If I die," said Wolf Rider, "it will be a good death. But if I live… no more war."

Shouts of anger and protest rang out.

"And if she would have me," Wolf Rider yelled, "if she would have me…I will ask for your daughter's hand in marriage."

The protests were drowned out by laughter. A jeering kind of laughter. Mocking.

If Wolf Rider was bothered by it, he did not show it. "After the Daybreak Star," he said, "before the moon rises again, I will return. I lost my honor once. Now there is only one way to win it back. I was delivered to make peace."

"He lies!" shouted Snake Boy. "He was delivered by me! Not a god!"

Quanah raised both hands, silencing the crowd. "Marriage? You must think we are fools. If we let you go, we will never see you again." He turned and, with a look of loathing, asked his daughter, "You would marry this man? This Pawnee?"

She stood quietly, her face calm, without a hint of emotion.

It was only one movement. One simple movement. But the effort required was vast.

She nodded, slowly—once.

The crowd gasped—some in horror, some in disgust.

With a doubting look in his eye, the chief leaned closer, glaring at the prisoner. "How do I know your words are true?"

Once again Wolf Rider lowered his head, indicating a leather badge hanging from his neck. On it was a beaded symbol of the sun. "I wear the mark of the Morning Star, *Ti-ra-wa*, the One Above. I will not lie to him."

The chief slowly brought the knife up and rested the tip of the blade under Wolf Rider's chin. "It is *your* god, not ours!" He pushed the knifepoint deeper, almost puncturing skin. "We shall see." He turned to the crowd and said, "*Loo-ah*! Go! No one is to give him food or water. And you, Pawnee, we will see what kind of man you are."

With long, powerful strides, the mighty Quanah marched off, leaving the prisoner tied to the pole—alone.

Chapter 20

HE WAS STARTLED AWAKE BY SNARLING, GROWLING, and the snapping of teeth.

Wolf Rider opened his eyes to find a great clashing and heaving of bodies in a fierce struggle to the death, two dogs in the throes of such viciousness it was sickening to watch. Both were large, slavering at the mouth. One was black, the other brown, each dominant in their own right. They waged an inevitable battle over a scrap of food, the desires of a female during mating time, or maybe it was a simple matter as supremacy. Which dog was stronger, the better fighter.

They flew at each other in a blind rage again and again, maneuvering, looking for that one opening, an edge, however small, to assert itself. The black one lunged for the throat. The brown one reacted in more in defense of itself. And lost. The move was quick and decisive. A well-placed attack found the jugular. Teeth sank deep, and pulled. Blood gushed from its neck and down the animal went, writhing, shrieking, wailing in violent spasms of agony, then crying and whimpering as those spasms turned into twitches. Finally, there was no movement at all. The dog was lying lifeless in a pool of red while the victor licked the blood from its mouth. So savage and unexpected was the brutality, Wolf Rider feared for his life because there was nothing he could do to protect himself.

What came next was even more appalling. Before the brown one went down, a pack of dogs closed around them, crouching, watching, ears laid back, waiting for an opportunity, waiting for one or the other to lose its advantage, to let down its defenses and be at the mercy of the other. But there was no mercy between either of the two. Once the defeated animal was prone and unmoving, the pack unleashed its fury.

They sprang all at once, ignoring the much-feared victor, and leapt upon the dead animal, tearing and ripping at its flesh. In the midst of all of this, they turned on each other, nipping and biting, lunging and thrashing in an orgy of madness—fed by rabid hunger.

Only whips could separate them. Whips and grass switches and men who, by use of force and fierce determination, crushed the violence and stopped the beasts before they could destroy themselves. One of them had to be put down with a spear—so aggressive was its assault on the others. The rest went whimpering and snarling, limping and bleeding with tongues hanging to the far reaches of camp where they would lick their wounds and whine pitifully in pain. To all who witnessed it, the blood-brawl was disturbing, not so much because of the violence, but because of a growing fear the dogs were diseased. Not all. Just a few. But the few impressed the many. And suspicion fell on the lot.

Wolf Rider found little rest after the dogs fought. On those rare occasions when he did sleep, he was more vulnerable to attack, like a piece of meat hanging from a tree, waiting to be gorged upon. When awake, his aches seemed to grow with each passing moment. Discomfort became full and wide-spread agony. Cramps became sores. And sores, misery. Each and every condition went through a cycle of phases, from severe to a bearable kind of pain and back again, always faster, more intense than before. The range of symptoms, and of emotions, was enormous, as if the body was feeding on itself in a frantic search for food, rest, and water.

Between hunger and thirst, thirst was the most critical. After going several days without water, he knew there was a real danger of dying. Sweat no longer insulated the body. The cold mountain air penetrated deeper. And without freedom of movement, his body lacked the circulation needed to keep from freezing.

To look at him was to see a man whose strength and vitality had been utterly stripped away. Like a tree sagging, limbs drooping, his skin and bones felt like they were no longer a solid mass, but an affectation.

He tried in vain to find a position that was acceptable. If he squatted, the blood was cut off, his legs would go numb, and he had great deal of difficulty recovering from it. If he stood up straight, his body could not relax enough to where he could sleep. Eventually, he found a position he could tolerate at least for a while, one where he leaned forward, allowing his arms to take the brunt of his weight as he slept—or attempted to. Even then, the strain on his arms became too great and he had to constantly alter his posture.

Of course, the most difficult thing he had to deal with was the cold. Exposure worried him the most. His hands and face were left uncovered. He could feel the sting of frost on his skin, a burning sensation in his hands, especially the fingertips. If the weather got any colder, he was sure he would lose his fingers or possibly his hands, even if he survived.

Despite everything, he was not ready to give up. Not just yet. Invariably, when he was the most distraught, he turned to prayer. Time and time again, however, his prayers were interrupted. He became the victim of countless taunts, insults, and threats, often coming from young boys who spit at his feet, counted coup with their hands, or flailed him with grass switches. A few even took up lances and, with the blunt ends, thrust the tips at his eyes, chest, loins, and thighs, giggling as they did so, never striking him, yet near enough to be a source of constant irritation.

Throughout the day Cloud Wing watched from afar, biding her time. Twice she had to chase the boys away. As much as her father would allow it, she kept an eye on the prisoner, but eventually Quanah found ways around that by ordering her to do things she ordinarily didn't have to do.

On and on the game was played. Children and sometimes adults would tease and harass him by flicking water at his face or eating meat right in front of him. They would let the juices run down their chins, chewing and grinning, as they swallowed the sweet succulence of deer, rabbit, and raw liver, all of it intended to provoke…to make him slobber and beg.

But Wolf Rider would neither slobber nor beg, nor ask for mercy. He would close his eyes or hold his head high and just stare at his tormentors, pretending no one was there. More often than not, they came away bored or frustrated, amazed they could excite no response at all. After awhile, word soon spread of the *'Pawnee made of stone'* who could not be intimidated. And he was left alone.

* * *

Deep into the night, a cold winter wind came whipping through the valley, and it began to snow.

Worried by the sudden turn of weather, Cloud Wing was unable to sleep. She walked softly from her tepee. As the moon broke through the clouds, she stood before him, disturbed by what she saw.

His head was hanging. Strands of limp hair fell in disarray across his face, and over him was a light coating of snow. He appeared to be dead. Beneath the hair, however, there was a slight stirring. His lips were quivering, his teeth chattering, as small wisps of breath escaped from his mouth. She believed he was on the verge of freezing to death.

So she went to her tepee and returned a short time later, holding a blanket. As she stood before him again, an astonishing thing happened. He moved. He raised his head, as if awakened by her presence. Her feet made no sound at all, yet somehow he knew she was close by.

Slowly, he opened his eyes and stared at her. Nothing more. He barely had the strength to do that.

She approached and, with her fingers, dusted the snow from his shoulders, then gently pushed his hair aside so she could see his face. She draped the blanket around him, tugging neatly here and there, until it fit just right and was wrapped around him completely. With her left hand, she reached down, scooped up a handful of fresh snow, held it to his lips, and watched him take it into his mouth. He did it quietly, sucking at the flakes, cherishing each scoop as his tongue and mouth reveled in the moisture and water dripped down his throat. Then she fed him *pimmican*, a mixture of corn and meat, and watched him chew each morsel as if it were his last, never saying a word. He delighted in the fact he had something to eat. A gleam came to his eye, growing brighter with each chew. The more sustenance he took in, the better he looked. It was miraculous—the transition. One moment he was on the verge of starvation, suffering from frostbite and thirst. The next he was smiling.

The process, of course, was not all food and water. Much of it had to do with Cloud Wing and loving care she provided. Back and forth she went, offering him corn, then snow, corn, then snow, and he ate and drank, ate and drank until he had enough. And when the food was gone, she removed the blanket, opened her coat, placed her warm, soft body against his, repositioned the blanket, and slid her arms around him, holding him tight. And together, as the snow fell and wind blew and cold night air whirled about them, they remained in an embrace.

From his tepee, the Comanche chief watched. He grunted and went back to bed.

When morning broke the next day, everyone was amazed to find that Wolf Rider had somehow survived the night. But his state of health was of no concern to them. The thing they needed was food. The hungry looks on everyone's faces, the aggression of the dogs, the slow winter months without corn, all of these things pointed to a scarcity of food. So tribal leaders decided to organize a hunt. At the south side of camp where the prisoner was held, they gathered in groups to discuss strategy. Since the Comanches came from the southern plains, they had limited experience hunting in the mountains. Buffalo was their primary source of food, not elk or deer, so they argued about the most efficient methods to use and where they could find the most deer.

"Fire Mountain," a raspy voice said.

The hunters turned.

Wolf Rider whispered hoarsely, "Between Fire and Eagle Mountains, half a day's walk from here, you will find deer."

They couldn't believe an outsider would dare speak to them, let alone suggest a place where they might hunt. He received looks that could kill. Many told him to keep quiet. Words were shouted, names called, and he was rudely addressed.

The Comanche chief, however, seemed interested in what he had to say. "This place," he said, "between Fire and Eagle Mountains, you know of it?"

"Yes," replied Wolf Rider. "There is a lake where White-tails run through meadows of pine." He waited. No one objected. To the contrary, everyone was listening, so he described the area around Rainbow Lake and told them how to find it. He remembered it was near a waterfall, the place where a Comanche war party once tried to ambush him, but said nothing of it.

Even though it came from an outsider, a Pawnee, the suggestion was met enthusiastically. Hunters, chiefs, and members of Council discussed strategy again. They quarreled about who would go where and whether the men should hunt individually or in groups.

Almost as a joke, the Comanche chief turned to Wolf Rider and said, "And you…if you were a chief, what would you do?"

"If I were a chief," said Wolf Rider, "I would have one party go one place. A second, another. The strongest of arm and quickest with arrow, I would put upwind at the head of the valley, behind rocks and trees. The rest, those who are fastest of foot I would scatter in a long line and have them move slowly forward. They would start from far away, make as much noise as they could, and chase the elk and deer to the other end of the valley." He looked around to see if anyone was listening. They were listening closely. "That is what I would do," he said, "…if I were chief."

For a moment there was silence. They gawked at him, not knowing what to say. Before long they were engaged in a loud and excited discussion. Apparently they liked what they heard because the 'strongest of arm' and 'quickest with arrow' were chosen and those who were 'fastest of foot' were relegated to roles as chasers.

Chapter 21

IN HIS DESPERATE STRUGGLE TO STAY ALIVE, sleep became his only salvation. Mad with hunger, weak, and tormented by the wind and cold, Wolf Rider kept dozing in and out.

During the night, he heard dogs barking as shadowy figures hurried about the village. By the light of the campfires he could see drags being harnessed to dogs and gear laden and lashed to the poles. He remembered Cloud Wing coming to him, tucking the blanket tight around his shoulders, and whispering words of encouragement in his ear. For this she was reprimanded by her father, ordered not to go near the *pi-ta'-da* again. She then joined the others as an archer no less and in the process had undergone a complete transformation. She clothed herself in leggings and waistcoat like a man, and braided her hair to look like a man and strode off confidently when they left.

Up the snowy trails in the dead of night the hunting party trudged—dogs, men, and squaws. The women were given the task of slaughtering and butchering the deer. Through a mist of snow they climbed, leading to the mountain ranges to the east, toward Eagle and Fire Mountains, where 'White-tails ran through meadows of pine.'

Twice, maybe three times during the night Wolf Rider slept. By morning, when he woke up, the weather had improved significantly. The sun shined brighter. The warmer it grew. The snow began to melt and push aside the dismal gray clouds in favor of a clear-blue sky. Winter was shedding its ghostly dreariness. From it sprang the richness and promise of a new season.

Birds by the thousands, from swallows to larks to wrens, were migrating in flocks that seemed to flit through the sky day and night. Squirrels chattered. A flock of geese flew in formation, honking as they worked their way north. Buried deep in its den, a bear, having roused itself from its winter sleep, exercised its well-rested voice by giving out with a ferocious growl heard from mountaintop to mountaintop.

All throughout the valley the traces of spring abounded. From the dance grounds, however, came no sounds, no rustle of movement. Women and old men sat by the campfires, waiting…in anticipation of another feast. Outside the camp, alongside a creek, children played games. Others went sledding in the snow, using elk and buffalo bones as makeshift sleds, sliding downhill along an open trail. High atop the mountains—north, east, south, and west—smoke rose from campfires where sentries stood guard.

Wolf Rider viewed the smoke as his last sign of hope. Of the basic signals, only one served as a warning against attack and nothing short of an invasion by his fellow Pawnees could release him from the bonds of imprisonment. Otherwise, he was doomed and he knew it.

His will to live was just about broken. For some time now, considering his failing health and how he had been treated the last two days, he had resigned himself to the fact that he was going to die. Only two questions remained—*when* and *by what method*. If the Comanches were anything like the Pawnees, two or three things were likely to happen before that. It began with isolation, separating him from everyone else. Indifference, a lack of attention came next. At some point, he believed, he would be visited by a holy man, a medicine-healer, and made ready for the execution, if he didn't die of hunger or thirst first.

Techniques varied. Death by fire. Arrow, knife, spear. Strangulation. Drowning.

Or he would simply waste away. Cease to exist by neglect.

The possibilities were endless. Some deaths were slow, some fast, and some painful, too grisly to think about. He saw what they had done to his friend, War Hawk, and shuddered at the thought of the horrible way he was brutalized. Among the Comanches, torture seemed a favorite way of killing. If Wolf Rider had to die, he preferred something swift, like an arrow through the heart, yet somehow, given their sadistic nature, he expected the worst.

He prepared for it by doing what he had always done—singing and praying and admonishing himself for any wrongdoings he may committed, especially against the *Nabu'rac, Spirits of the Shadow Land,* or *Thunder Beings* who lived up high. If he had slain a deer and not given thanks to the spirit for the taking of its life, he was sorry. If he had shot a bird and not shown his appreciation, he begged its forgiveness. Soon he was praying to all the birds and beasts and to their spirits he asked to be exonerated for any wrongs he had done.

Even after all of this, he still felt at a loss, still felt an emptiness inside, but it had nothing to do with the lack of food.

What he was feeling was fear—fear of the unknown. Throughout his life he was told that when he died, he would journey into a state of darkness and emerge, body and spirit, in the realm of the dead, only with greater powers and the ability to influence the living. Although he considered himself a highly spiritual man, he still had his doubts, which led to a number of darker feelings—self pity, sorrow, shame. But never before had he suffered from such cruel and lasting deprivation.

"Think of *visions…of voices and songs*," his father once told him. He tried again and again and again, but no visions, no voices came to him.

"And though you will become weak," Two Buffalo once explained, "in your weakness they will see that you are strong. A good heart and noble spirit are what you must show."

If weakness and tolerance to pain proved to be the measure of a man's strength, then Wolf Rider had reached a level incomprehensible to others.

He was taught—in life, there was no random act. Everything had a purpose. He believed his was to explore the depths of his emotions and from them he would arise intact. And to do that he tried to concentrate on those experiences, people, and facets of life he found the most meaningful. But Cloud Wing was gone and he was not as clear-headed or clear-sighted as he had hoped. Fact is, it had gotten to the point where he was losing his ability to focus, to think as well as to see, and could feel himself slipping further and further into a state of permanent decline, a condition from which, he feared, recovery was no longer possible. It was a struggle just to keep his eyes open, and he could feel himself drowsing…drowsing deeper, the twilight darkening.

Just then he heard the high-pitched cry of an eagle as it circled the valley. He looked up, trying to catch a glimpse of it. His eyes explored the air above and saw a black speck soaring against the blue of the sky. The eagle was flying east to west in search of prey.

He wondered—*how do you catch an eagle without hurting it*? Could such a thing be done? Was the idea the whim of a foolish old man?

As a source of food, the eagle had no particular appeal as far as he knew. No one hunted it for its flavor or because it was nourishing. An eagle was sacred, beyond simple gratification, something to be admired from afar.

Yet for the past month Wolf Rider gave it a great deal of thought, this notion of catching an eagle. The question posed a dilemma, one he had no idea how to solve. An eagle's senses were far too keen for it to be taken by surprise. Its nest, perched in a crevasse or at the top a mountain, was impossible to reach, so there had to be a trick to catching it, a way of outsmarting it.

Think—he said to himself. *Ah, what was that? A sound…*

The crunch of feet on wet snow alerted him.

To his left walked an *hatalli*, a maker of *ti-war'-uks-ti*,* a holy man who was old, wore a robe made of wolf pelts, a bonnet of black feathers, and had dots of white paint dripping down his face like teardrops. He carried a lance in one hand, a charm rattle in the other, and looked at Wolf Rider as if he were an oddity, a curiosity, tilting his head this way and that, studying him with narrow, squinting eyes.

Quietly, the *hatalli* reached in a bag tied to his waist and pulled out a handful of dust, which he sprinkled on Wolf Rider's feet and shoul-ders before he took one last handful and showered it over his head. Wolf Rider coughed and this seemed to amuse the *hatalli* greatly. Once the purification process was completed, the *hatalli* did a small dance, lightly shuffling his feet. He shook the rattle, jabbed at the air with the lance, and mumbled something. Occasionally, Wolf Rider understood a word or two, but little else. The intonations were rhythmic, like a chant, repeated again and again. Whatever the meaning, the gist was clear.

Wolf Rider was about to be sacrificed. And given the look of the *hatalli*, it was soon.

Two or three times the old man poked him with the spear and not once did Wolf Rider flinch or make a sound. His body was too numb, too ravaged by the elements to feel much of anything. His mind, how-

---

* magic

ever, seemed to be jarred awake. After several more pokes from the lance, he whispered hoarsely, "How do you catch an eagle, old man?"

The *hatalli* looked at him quizzically.

So Wolf Rider asked the question again.

The *hatalli* scratched his chin, raised his voice in anger. Either he did not know or care to talk. He threatened the prisoner with the spear and just walked away, muttering to himself.

Once again, Wolf Rider was left alone with his thoughts. As he had done so many times, he strained against the ropes and could feel no slackening in his wrists or ankles. If anything, the ropes had grown tighter, were cutting deeper into his skin.

There was no escape.

All he wanted to do now was sleep. He closed his eyes and pictured himself lying in a peaceful place, at home in *Tuh-parisu* next to a warm fire. Almost immediately he began to drift off, to lose himself to unconsciousness. He became less and less aware of the cold, less aware of everything as the world around him began to fade. There was no fighting it. No stopping it. No fear. No feelings. Just a vague understanding the end was near.

He surrendered to it completely.

*　*　*

When, at what particular moment in time, he had no idea.

Somewhere in that dark abyss between conscious thought and nothingness came a sound that pulled him back.

He woke up unable to see because the glare of the sun against the snow was so bright. Blinking, he titled his head as he listened. At the far end of the valley, echoing as though from a hollow, came the shrill yelps of dogs. He peered around, trying to adjust his eyes to the light. Gradually, he could see shapes evolving in the landscape—tufts of snow, tepees, trees. Squinting through a veil of tears and a kind of myopic haze, he noticed shadows moving in the distance—

At the base of the mountain, around a jutting curve of land bordered by pines, the hunting party converged, merging from several trails into one as if it were a race. There were about ten sleds in all, pulled by packs of scruffy black- and brown-haired dogs. Alongside them ran the *parisu*, the hunters and squaws, dressed in fur, numbering about four times as many as there were dogs. Men and women were shouting, laughing, snapping grass switches and cracking their whips, urging the dogs on while the dogs kept barking, driven by a lust for raw meat. Together, they pulled drag poles piled with venison, the blood-soaked remains of carcasses, shanks of bone, deer and elk skins, leaving a bloody trail in the snow.

From the village, they were greeted by cheers and a pounding of drums. People were singing, making the *tremolo*.

The hunters arrived home happy and smiling, waving pelts and animal hides over their heads, eager to indulge themselves in the riches of the hunt. They danced around the *kill sleds* in celebration while the women hugged their husbands and the sons and daughters their fathers and brothers.

In their enthusiasm, something happened. It started with a snowball, one innocent snowball, and escalated into a fight where the most playful of intensions turned suddenly wicked—

All of it directed at the prisoner.

Men were hurling snow at him, packing handfuls of wet, soggy snow and not flinging it at him. Throwing! As hard as they could. From short range. The impact was devastating. His head and body were beaten senseless. He began to lose consciousness again. Finally, someone intervened. She thrust herself into the fray, pushing and shoving people aside, yelling at them to stop. So vocal and passionate was she, the entire camp froze and looked at her. And what they saw was a woman dressed in a man's clothes, wielding a tomahawk, slashing wildly this way and that, never intending to harm anyone, but close enough to make a point. The power of her strokes could have easily cleaved an arm from a shoulder or split a skull wide open. And almost immediately, once the snowballs started, they stopped.

Cloud Wing stood inside the circle of hunters, panting heavily, tomahawk raised, daring anyone to approach.

No one approached.

Not until her father came forward. He eyed the men with contempt and scolded them for what they did, then turned to Cloud Wing and cried, "*Loo-ah!* Go! No one will harm him any more."

And, with a dismissive wave of his hand, he sent everyone scattering to their lodges.

Cloud Wing, however, refused to leave. From her waistcoat she removed a leather sash, dabbed it in snow, and patted it against Wolf Rider's battered face.

Chapter 22

"The woman had magic to stir a man's blood."

— origin unknown

IT WAS PART WOLF, PART MONGREL. Like its ancestors of the wild, it had a highly evolved set of instincts when it came to potential prey. It was careful in selecting what it would eat. Man was not usually a part of its diet. The opportunity to partake of an easy victim, however, made it very tempting. Considered one of the more aggressive of those in the camp, the dog had been watching him for some time. It crouched, crept closer soundlessly, waited, crept closer, ears flat, head bent low, eyes never wavering. The man never moved. Yet the dog was still suspicious of him.

Ten feet away, it slinked forward again, then held back, sniffing to see if he was still alive. Nearer and nearer it approached, one nervous and quiet step at a time, cautious, motivated by something beyond hunger—an urge, the thrill of the kill. Only the victim, from the looks of things, appeared to be dead. The dog seemed aware of it, too. It raised its head, leaned closer, and smelled the man's feet. He was slumped against a pole, legs tucked beneath him, head down, hanging. From his thighs to the tips of his moccasins the animal sniffed up and down, once, twice, and, without warning, suddenly lunged, having judged the man dead, the body cold, or in such a weakened condition he was helpless. Its teeth bit down on something leathery and soft, nipping a part of his skin in the process.

Wolf Rider was shocked into consciousness, not so much because of the pain, but because of the shock and assault upon his body. He screamed, jerked his right leg back while the fangs still gripped the leggings just above the knee. He was completely at the mercy of the animal. Without use of his arms and legs, he couldn't defend himself or deliver any kind of counter blow. All he had was a fading glimmer of hope and the terror of knowing that he might be eaten alive, piece by piece. A pack of ravenous dogs stood close by, watching and waiting, anxious to join in the feeding frenzy should it come to that. Wolf Rider thrust his legs together as hard as he could, and the dog, aware that there was still fight left in the man, drew back with the leggings still clutched in his mouth. Snarling, it shook its head and tore away a portion of the leather from his thighbone to his ankle, and released it when it realized, instead of flesh, it had only bitten through the man's clothing. The dog didn't retreat so much as it did reassess the situation. It stood facing him, baring its teeth, growling, salivating, eyes fixed, crazed with hunger.

And Wolf Rider looked the creature straight in the eye, snarled, bared his own teeth, and growled menacingly, and did so with such conviction and evil intention, the dog appeared to be intimidated. It had no idea the man was powerless, incapable of doing it harm. All it understood was what its cousins of the wild understood, that men were capable of very bad things. To fight them was seldom done. Given no other choice, the consequences were disastrous if they did, ending with a wicked blow to the head, or something far worse. Yet when Wolf Rider growled, the dog expected him to attack or to make a threatening move in his direction. He did neither of these things. Instead, he held back and the dog saw a sign of weakness in the man's eyes—desperation and fear—a type of fear an opponent displays when it, when *he*, is unsure of himself, when he is no longer the master, superior in strength, or the fight has gone the other way.

With renewed intensity, the dog reasserted itself and snarled even louder. It bristled. It curled its lips, growled, snapped its teeth, and crouched closer as saliva dripped from its mouth. Wolf Rider had seen that look in an animal's eyes before, that wild, lustful glare when it was ready to attack, only this time it was not a panther, but a starved dog gone mad, a meat-eater whose prey was but for the taking.

Wolf Rider somehow knew it would come to this. Ever since the dog fight to the death, he realized the dogs in camp suffered from some type of disease—a disease that can easily be transmitted when a dog bites and punctures the skin. Eventually, the victim becomes infected. He catches a fever, goes mad, and dies a slow, painful death. Wolf Rider had seen it happen. And now he faced a meat-eater poised with that lustful glare, a malevolence that would stop at nothing. It crept closer, eyeing him as it growled, hind legs taut, ready to pounce.

Suddenly, a rock struck the dog as it opened its jaws. Every muscle in its being spasmed, recoiled from the strike. The dog yelped and all manner of distemper vanished in an instant—the curled lips, the look of wildness, the menacing glare—all of it gone, wiped from its face by one well-aimed throw.

"Go away!" a woman yelled. "Go!" In she rushed, carrying not a weapon, but a bearskin, which she snapped and flogged at the dog. "Go away!" she screamed.

The dog reacted with a half-hearted snarl before jumping back, avoiding the snap of the bearskin and avoiding the woman whose intensions were perfectly clear. Despite all of its fury, the dog became submissive. It leapt back, crouching, the hairs on its neck standing on end, then, all at once, turned and, with its tail tucked between its legs, slinked off quietly into the campgrounds, denied of the food it so desperately sought.

After it was gone, Cloud Wing looked at the pathetic condition Wolf Rider was in—the tattered leggings, the limp bedraggled hair, the fallow color of his skin, the lifeless look in his eyes—and cringed. She uttered a cry of anger and expressed her frustration by groaning and stamping her foot while seeing the man she loved slowly wither away—a man in such terrible shape, she could barely look at him, and when she did, the guilt was too much to bear. What her people were doing to him was senseless. It was torture and she resented it—so much in fact, she considered untying him right then and there and suffering the consequences of her actions. She knew her father was stern and vindictive. She couldn't go against him if she wanted to remain a Comanche. She could argue in his behalf, however, so with that in mind she hurried away, wiping the tears from her cheeks, dragging the bearskin behind her.

Wolf Rider didn't see the tears. He didn't see much of anything any more. He was only half aware of his surroundings. His ability to think and see and comprehend had become clouded. He knew she had saved his life—for the moment anyway—but, in his weakened state, things had become muddled. Things that were real seemed the stuff of dreams while he confused dreams with reality. The incident with the dog seemed almost like a figment of his imagination until he looked down and saw the torn leggings and the blood trickling down his shinbone.

It was only a matter of time now. Sooner or later the dog would return hungrier, more determined than ever. If not that dog, then another—madder, leaner, more vicious. And no one would be around to save him.

He had a sudden impulse to break free. Many times he tried to rub the ropes that bound him against the pole, intending to escape that way. He scraped and scraped and scraped. But it was hopeless. The ropes weren't even close to wearing through. The skin around his thumbs and wrists, however, were rubbed raw and bleeding. Because of that he had to quit.

No food meant there was nothing to replenish his energy; no water meant no fluids to protect the body. And he was in short supply of each.

He felt no sensation in his legs other than a tingling numbness that comes when the blood ceases to flow. In spite of the lack of feeling and mobility, when he went to stand, there was a sudden throbbing at his knees and lower back. Down he slumped, in the same position as before. Since the circulation had been blocked, the muscles were rendered useless. They had a deadness to them.

He was tempted to sit there, do nothing, and just give up. In some respects, he wanted to die. He welcomed death. Prayed for it. But he was both persistent and stubborn and neither would allow it.

Dragging his legs a little at a time, he managed to flatten his feet against the ground and gain some leverage. Squatting, he waited for the blood to circulate. He leaned against the pole, flexed his knees, pushed, and rose ever so slightly, only to have his legs give out. After resting for a moment, he pushed again. Up, up, up. By the tiniest of margins he rose, straining, groaning, giving it everything he had. With one final push, he fought through the pain, stood up, and slowly lifted his head. And through drooping eyes he saw—

A campgrounds that was quiet and still as the first rays of sunlight spilled over the mountains. In the distance, he heard a man and a woman arguing, talking back and forth, but the wind and the baying of wolves drowned them out. So he closed his eyes and heard nothing more.

When he opened his eyes again, it was late afternoon and he saw an entirely different campgrounds, one that was bustling with activity. The improved weather and success of the hunt helped to create a livelier, more festive atmosphere. People were scurrying every which way at once. The scent of roasting meat filled the air as women stood around a campfire spouting flames as tall as those who stood around it. He saw young girls with a single feather braided into their hair, walking around, smiling, braiding a single feather into everybody else's hair—young men, old men, maidens, squaws.

To his disappointment, Cloud Wing was nowhere to be found.

In her absence he noticed a tepee had been erected in the middle of the campgrounds. Painted along the skirt were a horse, elk, and buffalo; on the sides, symbols and other animals. To the west, facing him, were a Bow, Arrow, and Lightning, representing the *Thunder Beings*; to the south a Cornstalk and Leaves of the *Cleansing Sage*; to the north, above the entrance, a Flaming Rainbow. Of all the tepees he had ever seen, this was by far the most beautiful.

A dance area was cleared next to the tepee and everyone, having clothed themselves in their finest buckskins, gathered around it. Inside, the chiefs and member of Council met to exchange *kill talks* and ready themselves for the feast to follow. Outside, drums pounded like thunder. People sang songs, making the *tremolo*. And when the meeting was over, the leaders joined the rest of the revelers and they laughed and ate and sang and had a good time.

Food was brought in baskets and long wooden troughs. Ribs of elk, deer, *ka'wis*, livers, hearts, and flanks of meat, fresh from the fire, were greedily eaten, consumed with a voraciousness equal to a pack of starved wolves.

Wolf Rider watched with a fierce kind of envy. He could scarcely remember the taste of cooked meat. But, as he had done so often, he tried to put all thoughts of hunger out of his mind.

Just before dark, a Crier called everyone together, so they could hold a *kill dance*. Priests and holy men, the makers of *ti-war'-uks-ti*, once again sang songs and did the *tremolo* while moving their feet to the rhythm of the drums. A few dancers, naked to the waist, painted themselves red all over, with streaks of lightning running down their arms. Soon everyone joined hands around the campfire, making a *Sacred Hoop.*

Into their midst came more dancers, wearing animal hides. These were the Buffalo Dancers, the Dancers of the Wolf and Grizzly. Another was a mighty winged bird with long colored feathers hanging from its limbs. It swooped around the circle of people, gliding effortlessly. Even the Wolf and Grizzly gave way to the mighty Winged Bird as it imitated flight and swept into the darkness of night.

Wolf Rider watched with wonder, with eyes swollen half shut, witnessing a spectacle much the same as those performed by his own people. In it were the bestial dancers, the fiery spirits, the singing, the war whoops, the piercing shrieks, the pomp of ceremony, and joy of festivity.

On one occasion he decided to join in the chorus—quietly at first, no louder than a whisper. The harmony was simple, the melody basic, the words and music never rising beyond a mere chant. But as the tempo quickened, so did the fervor, as did the richness of Wolf Rider's voice. Tone, quality, resonance—everything grew dramatically. Drums pounded with mounting rhythm. Young girls and boys sang with inexhaustible enthusiasm; old men and squaws with youthful passion, the repetitious chant swept along by the relentless crashing of the drums. All of it building and building. As it did, the volume of Wolf Rider's singing kept rising as well. He matched them beat for beat, note for note, to the point where he was practically shouting at the top of his lungs—until all at once he realized both the drums and chanting had stopped.

Everyone was staring at him, jaws agape with brows furrowed.

The whole of the Comanche Nation was incredulous, not believing what they heard or saw—as if a ghost had come to life right before their very eyes.

With his strength virtually spent, bleeding, dying of thirst and hunger, Wolf Rider collapsed. He slumped against the pole, consoled by the fact… or hoping…that a new journey was about to begin—

The journey of death.

Chapter 23

AT THE HEIGHT OF THE FESTIVITIES, the Comanche chief stood up and said, "From the Red River of the North, I am Quanah, Chief of the Comanches. As our fathers spoke to us, I say to you…when we eat the meat of the deer, we gorge ourselves not on just its flesh, but on its strength and spirit. When we swallow the meat of the hawk, we devour the swiftness of its wings, the vengeance of its claws, the sharpness of its eyes. And when we taste the eagle, we will fly upon the battlefield with the power of an eagle and take into our clutches those who oppose us."

Suddenly, there was a raucous outpouring from the crowd, filled with jubilation and howling and yelling, all in support of Quanah.

"And of the flesh we have eaten," he cried, "we honor those who have satisfied our hunger. And upon the enemy we shall unleash our thirst for blood! We will kill the Pawnees! Trample them like buffalo running through the grass!"

Again, there was a strident roar from the crowd and more dancing, the bestial dancers mingling with the mighty Winged Bird, and those painted in red, mingling with the rest, all gyrating around in a circle, joined in the Sacred Hoop.

Many speeches were made at the conclusion of the feast. Pipes filled with *chacun sha sha*, the bark of the red willow, were passed among the leaders. As they smoked, they talked about the *Other World*, the *Spirit Lands*, about war and how many lives would be taken in battle, after which Giant Wolf was paraded around the campfire—led, of course, by Snake Man. Hands were painted on the sides of the horse, claiming ownership, and people hollered and laughed and called out to Snake Man, asking him to ride the Giant Wolf again.

Gamely, he tried.

In one easy hop, he threw himself on the animal's back, legs strad-dled, hands clutching the mane, without falling off or being thrown. Gi-ant Wolf stood with its head bowed as Snake Man sat proud and high, chest puffed out, hands on his hips, preening for everyone to see.

"Ride him!"—"Run him!"—"Show us, Snake Man!"—they shouted.

He kicked at the animal's sides, but the animal did not move or give any indication that it would. Everyone laughed. He tried it a second time, digging his heels into its flanks. Still the animal did not budge. And again there was laughter. As Snake Man thrashed at the horse, kicking and slapping at it, they heard a whistle, a soft, breathless blowing of air. Perhaps it was statement, the last sound a dying man could make.

Wolf Rider followed with a feeble, gasping call, "*Ka-coo! Ka-coo!*"

Giant Wolf bolted, head up, alert, tossing Snake Man from its back. The laughter was loud and infectious, but died when Snake Man rose angrily to his feet. The horse ambled to the edge of camp and halted by the side of the prisoner.

This incensed Snake Man all the more. With jaws clenched, he drew his knife, marched toward the horse, only to be stopped by Cloud Wing who warned him to leave the prisoner alone. She stood in his way, a formidable force to be reckoned with—eyes glaring, chest heav-ing, every muscle taut and flexed. Then Quanah walked up, saying he would not allow any quarrelling during the dance or after.

"*Loo-ah!* Go!" he demanded, then ordered Snake Man to his tepee and Cloud Wing to hers.

The dance continued long into the night—with Wolf Rider slip-ping closer and closer to death—until, finally, the campfires faded and everybody sought the warmth and comfort of their skin lodges.

As the winter wind blew from the north, a bitter cold returned and Wolf Rider could feel the first stages of frostbite begin to take hold. His leggings and leather coat were frozen stiff. He could hear a crisp rattling as he pulled at the ropes. And there was a sudden and desper-ate realization that at any moment his heart would stop and his suffer-ing would end.

He couldn't feel his hands at all. His legs felt rigid, like frozen stumps. He was beaten and knew it. He hung his head to allow the cold to penetrate while the world slowly dimmed around him. He felt an overwhelming sense of sadness, caused by an immense yearning for Cloud Wing. It was as if he were detached from himself and the sadness he felt was for another person.

He would die in the camp of her people. Alone. Broken-hearted. No one would miss him, or notice. He was a disease, an animal to be pitied, nothing more, and would go ignored now and in the afterlife, floundering in the *Spirit Lands*, the *Shadow Land*, because of the dishonor he had brought to himself and to the *Wolf Pa'ni*.

Later, when everyone was asleep, there was a commotion inside one of the tepees, an argument between two people. An older man and younger woman kept bickering, raising and lowering their voices, speaking of loyalties broken and fidelity to family. It was evident the older man was upset. He chastised the younger woman for her disobedience, yet she was strong-willed and determined not to give in.

Wolf Rider listened, but the words were lost in the wind and wolves howling from the forest.

He hunched his shoulders in an attempt to keep warm. Nothing else mattered any more. Warmth was the only thing that kept him alive and he had been denied it for…how long had it been? Two, three nights now? He couldn't remember. He found it harder and harder to do, to trick himself into believing he could survive on sheer will alone. Again, as he had done countless times, he closed his eyes. His entire body fell limp as he prepared for sleep, perhaps his last.

All at once everything stopped. The wolves. The wind. The two people arguing.

Out of the silence came the crunching of mocassined feet through the wet snow as someone approached. When the visitor spoke, it was with anger and bitterness—

"You said the Pawnees have never attacked the Comanches. So who raided our village and took my daughter? Who broke the legs of *Red Crow* and left him to die? Who attacked my people at *Grass Creek* and chased the buffalo from our lands?"

The voice moved around to his back. "Who took the scalps of my brother and fellow braves two summers ago?"

Wolf Rider felt some movement behind him, something touching his ankles.

Snap.

A piece of rope was cut.

"Who killed the *Sheyelas** at *Bull Run* in the *Winter-of-the-Snow-Blind*?"

Snap.

Another piece was cut. His feet were now free.

"And who killed the *Hunkpapa* and *Sioux* '*Where the Rivers Run Deep?*'"

Snap. Snap.

More ropes were cut.

He felt a loosening around his wrists.

"Who waged war against my father, Black Hand, and his father before him?"

Snap went the final rope binding his wrists.

Wolf Rider plunged face down into the snow, too weak to break the fall. His body bounced, then lay unmoving as the harangue continued, "And now the Pawnee claims it was Comanches who attacked them. A lie! You attacked us! You killed my brother and took the lives of many others! It was you, the Pawnee, who waged war against the *Hunkpapa*, the *Sheyelas*, and the *Sioux*!"

Wolf Rider could barely roll to his side, but he did. He rolled to his side, then to his back, and looked up, and standing above him was Quanah, eyes ablaze, hand gripping a long-bladed knife.

"You are free to go," shouted Quanah. "The Giant Wolf is waiting. But hear me, Pawnee. If you do not come back before the moon rises a day from now, the Comanches will attack the Pawnees!"

He motioned to someone. And out of the cold night stepped Cloud Wing, clutching a bearskin around her shoulders.

At the same time the chief slid his knife back in its sheath. "And my daughter will be driven from the village. She will wither and die, like a tree cut from its roots. She will go without food and water! This I promise, if you do not return."

Wolf Rider hardly had the strength to do anything. With all the effort he could muster, he raised himself to one knee and slowly, very-slowly stood on both legs, wobbling and teetering until he found his

---

* Cheyenne

balance, and shuffled his feet like an old man. Unsteadily, he struggled, bent over, doddering toward the horse, his hair hanging lankly down the sides of his face. Giant Wolf whinnied as he staggered closer. As hard as Wolf Rider tried, every attempt to straddle the animal failed. There was no spring in his legs; no strength in his arms; no ability to lift himself or climb onto its back. Cloud Wing tried to help, but Quanah shouted at her to stand back.

Wolf Rider clearly demonstrated that without any assistance he was incapable of mounting the horse. He stood, panting, leaning against its side, contemplating what to do. Just when Cloud Wing and Quanah thought he had given up, he brushed the animal's mane, stroked it, spoke to it soothingly in whispered tones.

Immediately, the horse lowered itself, got down on its haunches, bending its long, angular legs—front legs first, back legs next—until its back was even with his ribcage. He leaned over, chest and belly flopping onto its spine, resting on the curve of its back. He threw his right leg up and over, stretching, groaning, then sat erect.

"*Hun'ta!*" he commanded. "Up! Up!"

Giant Wolf responded by pushing up from the ground—hind legs first, forelegs next—raising itself with rider firmly seated in place. After a snap of the reins, the horse turned and broke into a trot. Wolf Rider held onto his mane, hunched over, riding as if he were half asleep.

Or dead.

Quanah watched in awe, trying not to show his admiration. Once the prisoner was gone, he called several warriors around him.

He pointed at two men clothed in buffalo skins, two men noted for being fast afoot and excellent trackers. Their names were *High Hawk* and *Shakopee*.

Quanah said to them, "Follow him. See where he goes."

Chapter 24

CLOUDS WERE GATHERING TO THE WEST—dark clouds, angry clouds—with a heaviness to them. The promise of more snow perhaps. A deeper cold, fraught with gloom.

Snake Man spent much of the night sharpening the arrow he would use to kill Wolf Rider. He scraped and ground the tip against a rock until it could slice leather by sheer touch, as a knife could…until his fingers were rubbed raw. And bleeding.

At the same time he sat praying and wondering about many things. What trick the Pawnee would employ. If he would return. The decision reached by his father. The conduct of a warrior.

He concluded the actions and fairness of each would be determined tomorrow. His was not to judge, just to execute.

Everything was made ready the day of the challenge. Quanah ordered all sentries to take their places around the village. At first sighting of the Pawnee he said they were to shoot fire arrows into the air.

Throughout the morning and afternoon the elders, priests, warriors, and members of Council sat in scattered groups, warming themselves by the fires, discussing the routine matters of the day. Whatever the topic, they always seemed to revert to the confrontation at dusk.

Snake Man, meanwhile, decorated his bow and arrow with feathers and painted his face and chest red to show his desire for blood. In spite of the weather, he wore no shirt, kept his chest bare to atone for himself, as a sign of strength and virility. Poised in his father's tepee, he waited.

Outside, his sister waited, too, with a bearskin wrapped around her shoulders, staring at the gathering clouds.

A holy man, holding a medicine rattle and branch of the *cleansing sage*, crawled from his Sweat Lodge to say—

"Long have I fasted, Father, so you may protect us. All night and all day I have bathed myself in holy water, here where the bear and mountain lion live, where the spotted eagle and hawk fly, where the two-leggeds, four-leggeds, and wings-of-the-air take shelter. This is my final plea. I have felt the warmth of the Sacred Fire, Father. Behold me! I have prayed to the Spirits of the Mountain, to the Spirits of the Wind, and to the Spirits of the Dead, yet I have not heard an answer. The night is past, the water gone, the fire dead, and I stand before you—my vigil ended. Do you hear me, Father? With a song of love, I sing to you."

With little variance of sound and tempo, he sang, "*Hey-ya hey. Hey-ya hey. Hey-ya hey…*"—shaking the rattle, moving his feet, never keeping still.

All around him fires were lit to accommodate the approaching nightfall. A drum pounded slowly, summoning the challenger. The beat was interrupted now and again as the drummer grew tired and his enthusiasm waned. Wolf Rider had not shown himself yet, and the sun was sinking, dipping below the peaks of the mountains, the light paling across the eastern sky.

In the center of camp stood a lone figure glaring at opposite ends of the valley, east and west. Brows furrowed, head bent forward, bear-like, Quanah was growing impatient—not only with Wolf Rider's return, but with the braves he had sent to follow. Urgently, he called to the sentries—

"Koowi-ki! Koowi-ki!"

But the sentries did not answer.

Suddenly, the drum stopped. In disgust, the drummer threw his baton down and went inside his tepee.

With long, lurching strides the chief lumbered across the dance grounds and yelled, "*Koowi-ki!*"

Everyone listened.

But still there was no answer.

Enraged, he turned and yelled again.

War cries rang out. Warriors raised their weapons and shouted, decreeing their vengeance on all Pawnees.

Cloud Wing felt a sudden stabbing in her heart. Two days from now, a month, two months, there was a good chance she would die alone in the wilderness by starvation, eaten by a black bear, or killed by an Arapahoe, a tomahawk driven into in her skull, savaged in a way she could not imagine, in ways only women can be savaged, forced against their will to commit some lewd act, only to be disposed of afterward. Yes, she was afraid, but not for herself.

If Wolf Rider did not return, there would be dire consequences to pay: a village would be plundered, men women would die, and unless something was done to break the cycle, each tribe would make continued attempts at retribution for years to come.

She wondered if she had misjudged the Pawnee. Did something happen to him? Was he too weak to travel? Were his intensions never to return? Could any Pawnee be trusted? What secret plot was he hatching?

She wasn't the only one thinking these thoughts.

Every Comanche had questions, had doubts.

Many believed war was imminent, that letting the prisoner go was a mistake, including Quanah.

He had risen to power because of his aggressive nature. Noted for being a relentless warrior, endowed with a good mind as well, he earned a reputation as a man not to be lied to, crossed, or misled in any way. His prowess in the field of battle was legendary. And he had the scars to prove it. His strength was evident in his massive arms and shoulders and the intense bearing with which he carried himself. In a fight he had few equals. He once defended himself against two Kiowas bare-handed; he broke one of their necks and tossed the other over the side of a cliff. Quanah was only sixteen at the time. Since then he had gained prominence as a leader and formidable opponent, never having been defeated in either role. But of his many skills, none surpassed his ability to motivate men into battle.

All eyes were fixed on him as he paced back and forth. All at once he stopped, raised his eyes slowly, leering like a madman. Acting upon some primal urge—

He incited. He provoked. He screamed. He called the warriors around him, wildly waving his arms, and told them to gather their weapons and prepare for war.

"Tomorrow we will attack the Pawnee!" he cried.

A deafening roar rang throughout the camp. Warriors were yelling, jumping up and down, lifting their shields, their spears, their battle axes and tomahawks, and shaking them, dancing in celebration. As they whooped and hollered, a distant shout sounded from a mountain—

"*Koowi-ki!*"

The shout was lost amid the celebration. But the sight that followed was not.

A fire arrow, launched from a bluff, sailed high over the trees like a shooting star. Warriors and chiefs fell silent as they looked at the bluff. Once again the dogs barked, but were quieted by the *kara-hus*, the old men, who snapped grass switches at the their backs until the dogs went whimpering, beaten, throughout the camp where they would curl up and lick their wounds in the shadows of the tepees.

Cloud Wing took two steps forward and froze, tightening the bearskin around her. Her concern was no longer for herself. She stared across the clearing expectantly. Anxiously.

In the stillness of the early evening came a noise, faint and distant, the scrape and patter of movement, of feet crunching through snow and ice, followed by a sudden calling of voices—"*Ah-eeeee!*"

Again, the dogs barked, but were hushed by the grass switches.

Half way down the mountain, among a thicket of pines, men were running. Now and again they could be seen dodging left and right, avoiding the trees as they hurried toward the valley. Both were bundled in heavy furs with turbans crowning their heads.

At last, High Hawk and Shakopee had returned!

Into the clearing they ran. They splashed through the stream, into camp where the white-skinned tents were scattered. They never slowed, never broke stride in their haste to get home. In spite of the cold, their faces were sweating, flushed from exhaustion. They staggered toward the fires and halted beside the chief, trying to catch their breaths.

"The Pawnee!" cried Shakopee, pointing. "The one who rides the wolf…he comes!"

There were moans of surprise, looks of skepticism and uncertainty.

Quanah scowled and drew back, unsure what to make of it. He turned and looked up at the mountain.

If someone looked hard enough, long enough, he could see just about anything moving through the trees. But the trails were deserted, the landscape barren of people, and of animals.

High upon a bluff, a distant shout echoed—

"*Koowi-ki!*"

Another fire arrow, arching across the dark sky, fluttered, leaving a trail of smoke.

The crowd turned and looked toward the bluff. First one person, then another, and another thrust out a hand, shouting, pointing at a place along the slope of the mountain where they thought they saw someone, only to find the trails deserted, merging with the shadows as nightfall drew near.

Along the slopes and majestic sweep of the High Country, each area was watched. From the peak of the far mountain to the base of the valley and everywhere in between, the challenger was nowhere to be seen.

Moments later, as if by magic, at the edge of the clearing, swathed in furs and turban headdress, Wolf Rider emerged from the trees and led Giant Wolf into the stream. As he reached the bank, once again the dogs began to snarl and bark, but were immediately silenced by the *kara-hus* who flogged grass switches at them.

In quick succession, from the campgrounds, Snake Man broke from his tepee, shirtless, streaked in red, eyes glowering at his intended victim.

At the other end, plodding steadily, hooves slogging through the ice-covered snow, Wolf Rider walked the horse into camp, taking his time, as if to say—*Here I am. I have kept my promise. Look at me! A Wolf Pa'ni. I have come to meet my death.*

Proud was the walk of the horse, legs bending, unbending at the knees, head bobbing up and down, tail swishing contentedly.

There was pride in rider as well—turban headdress pulled low over his forehead, covering his ears, shoulders raised, back straight, hands softly gripping the reins.

Finally, he stopped and dismounted slowly, grimacing as his feet hit the ground. One eye was shut, his face swollen and bruised. And when he took his first few steps, he had a pronounced limp in his left leg. A foot was dragging, his knee buckling at the joint. Awkwardly, he hobbled for ten steps or so, then let go of the horse's reins, and stood still, trying to conceal the obvious pain he was in. One hand hung loose at his side. The other grasped the front of his coat.

There seemed to be a recklessness about him, a fearlessness, as if he viewed the moment with hidden joy. Instead of being frail, having gone days without eating, his body looked thick and massive under the coat, as though his chest had been bloated from his infirmities. His condition, apart from being slightly hideous, was pitiful. Yet beneath it all he was brash, not lacking in guile whatsoever.

In the center of camp he waited—under the watchful glare of the chief and every man, woman, and child who called himself a Comanche.

Three hundred people stood watching, and waiting.

Snake Man advanced, taking long, confident strides, hair greased back, head held high, a proud, imperious figure, with red marks painted across his bare chest, streaks of red and black smeared on his cheeks below the eyes. For a young man barely removed from boyhood, the effect was startling. It made him look bigger, bolder, stronger.

He stopped forty paces from his victim. They looked at one another—eyes steady, faces hard. The recklessness Wolf Rider once displayed had now disappeared. Gone, too, was the sympathy Snake Man may have had for his enemy.

For one brief moment Wolf Rider glanced at Cloud Wing. And she at him. He felt a peculiar kind of contentedness, knowing if he was going to die, it would be with a final, lasting impression of her.

He could feel his heart ramming against his ribcage, a sense of inevitability.

He recalled the day nine months ago when he faced the Council and sought permission to strike out on his own, a day which grew from a simple rite of passage into a life-changing event.

He remembered the Comanches setting the grass on fire. The buffalo plunging into the river. The Long Grass crackling. Ghosts rising from the smoke. Running all day and all night. The pride in knowing that *Tuh-parisu* had been saved from certain ruin.

He remembered seeing Giant Wolf for the first time. Learning how to ride. Going for days without seeing another person, without seeing a *taraha*, the clumsy brutes, all shaggy and thumping through the grass, their hooves trampling like drums.

He remembered a dream, a vision of giant wolves galloping. *Dark clouds! Angry clouds! And blood upon the land!* Sleeping on a bluff beside a young woman. The secret urges and secret desires she aroused in him. How his breath was taken away by the beauty of the Heads of the Ancient Stones. Discovery of a vast and mysterious new world.

The *Wasichus*. Men of pale skin who carried sticks of lightning, shot thunder, and rode upon strange-looking tepees pulled by packs of giant wolves.

He remembered the people, places, and events that influenced him—

Secret Pipe, the cave, his paintings. The Paducahs. The weddings. Dancing all night. The grisly way War Hawk had died. Smoking *chacun sha sha* with the Yumas. The wicked chief, *Ik-tome*, and the Snake People.

The deprivation, the purging, and cleansing of his spirit. Traveling alone from *Tuh-parisu* to the Shiny Mountains and beyond, to regain his shadow.

Through it all, one person stood above all the rest.

From her, the *Nabu'rac*, his mother and father, *Ti-ra-wa*, the *Opirikut*—from these he drew inspiration.

Now he was ready to face one more challenge, perhaps the most dangerous yet.

He took a deep breath, looked at Snake Man.

And Snake Man at him.

There was silence—silence everywhere.

The dogs sat still, licking their wounds.

Overhead, an eagle flew, a dim ghost in the gray light of dusk. It rode a gust of wind, soared one moment, swooped the next. During its final pass, it screeched, then by some stroke of magic vanished into the twilight.

One final glance from Wolf Rider—at the fading specter above, then at Cloud Wing—and there wasn't anything left to do.

He released his grip on the coat and shrugged. The coat slipped from his shoulders, fell in a rumpled mass to the ground.

Snake Man flinched—as did Quanah—as did everyone else.

Throughout the village there were mutterings of confusion, startled gasps, murmured groans. Everyone stared at the Pawnee, amazed, as if to say—

What manner of trickery is this?

Beneath the coat was a golden, Spanish breastplate. The Comanches had no idea what it was, or what it was supposed to be. It had ripples where the belly was flat, two round impressions where the chest muscles were. When Wolf Rider lightly tapped the surface of it, it sounded like stone.

"Here!" he cried. "Kill me, Snake Man! If you can…"

Snake Man didn't say a word. He took four steps forward, placed the arrow in his bow, narrowed his eyes, and breathed deeply. He wasn't worried about missing the target. At forty paces, he could hit a rabbit as it scurried through the grass. His hesitation, rather, came from someplace else—not indecision, but by the manner and behavior of his opponent who stood defenseless, hands at his sides, without a trace of fear, as if wanting…expecting to die.

Was he crazy? What type of man would deliberately face his own execution?

Then, almost imperceptibly, there was a slight change, a slight upturn of the lips, the crease of a smile from the Pawnee, defying him. *Mocking him*!

The arrogance! The impudence! The insanity of it!

What kind of fool would smile before taking an arrow through the chest?

Snake Man felt a rush of anger, his pulse quickening, the blood coursing through his body.

There was no reason to wait.

Gritting his teeth, he cocked the bowstring back, raised the bowstring and feathers to his cheek, sighted the mark, and, as he let go, shouted—

"Die, *pi-ta-da*!"

The arrow darted away. Plunged. Struck true, puncturing the stone shirt.

Wolf Rider fell to his knees, blood pouring from beneath the armor.

The Comanches watched to see if he would get up. A dog barked as he rolled to his knees. He winced, clutched both hands around the shaft of the arrow, then pulled. The shaft broke. He weakened for a moment, leaning off balance, then propped himself up, and stood.

Everyone groaned.

They watched him lift the metal breastplate above his head and throw it down.

"I live, Comanche!" he said, walking forward, limping, dragging a foot.

He grabbed Snake Man's bow and snapped it in half across his knee.

Snake Man looked at the Pawnee's torn shirt, at a gaping hole where it was punctured by the arrow. He saw a broken piece of shaft protruding from Wolf Rider's chest, the arrowhead embedded, blood trickling from the wound.

He couldn't believe the Pawnee was still alive.

Wolf Rider turned and yelled toward the mountain, "*Hoy-ah-hh!*"

Fire arrows whistled through the air, announcing a small party of strangers who were approaching the village.

Wolf Rider gestured to the west. With a half grimace, half smile, he said "Some of my people…to meet my brother, Snake Man. They are coming to celebrate my marriage."

They say there is a moment in a man's life which lives in his heart and mind forever, when he is sustained by joy and emotion, when food and water and other things cannot sustain him, and he is strengthened by one experience that will burn everlasting like a fire within him.

This was one of those moments.

Cloud Wing rushed up and hugged him in her arms. Wolf Rider was glad that she did. He realized he couldn't remain on his feet much longer. From a pouch tied to his waist he removed a necklace of panther teeth.

"Here," he said. "They are the only teeth an old man can give."

Puzzled, she looked at him. "Old? You are not old."

Wolf Rider laughed. It hurt. "I am not old," he replied, "but the man who taught me *hozho* was."

"*Hozho?*"

He nodded, grinning weakly. "Yes, *hozho*. You are my…*hozho*."

Finally, he fell into her arms again.

That was the night Wolf Rider became known as *Peacemaker*, husband to Cloud Wing. The Comanches accepted him as one of their own. The Pawnees admitted him back into the tribe, and the two tribes entered into a treaty, which lasted longer than the lifetime of their common leader—

A man named Peacemaker, chief of the *Wolf Pa'ni*.

Epilogue

*"A strong man…a good man, a wise and
clever man, one swift afoot who can see all—
he is a man who will one day be chief."*

– Secret Pipe

YEARS LATER, a man once known by several names stood with his grandson at the base of a mountain, looking up at the sky. What he saw was a revelation, an inspiration. He had spent most of his adult life trying to accomplish something most people would consider foolish, an act that served as a source of inspiration for much of his life. It reminded him of his youth, yet, as a practical matter, served no purpose other than being one of the few remaining things he hoped to accomplish before he died.

Having seen this revelation, he and his grandson, Born-of-Water, a boy ten winters old, mounted their horses and rode north, away from the mountain. Eventually, Born-of-Water asked, "Where are we going, grandfather?"

The man once known as Flying Fox, Wolf Rider, and now Peacemaker replied "We are going to visit the Cheyenne, to buy a shovel."

"A shovel?"

"Yes. A tool they bought from the *Wasichus*."

"What do we need a shovel for?"

"To dig a hole."

They rode a little farther before Born-of-Water asked, "Why a hole?"

"You shall see," was all Peacemaker said.

Farther along the trail, Born-of-Water remarked, "I do not like the *Wasichus*. Their food is chewy, their clothes soft. When we wear their clothing, it makes us weak. And when they speak, they say crooked things. Why are the *Wasichus* so mean?"

"Not all *Wasichus* are mean. Not all."

"They say more are coming, like locusts in summertime. So many it is impossible to count them all. And when they come, all Indians will die."

"Not *all* Indians. Some of us will learn how to survive…those who are clever like a fox."

Later that morning, after visiting the Cheyenne, they returned to their village. When they arrived, many family members and friends greeted them, including Cloud Wing who, despite her age, was still beautiful. Beside her stood a group of children, all of whom smiled upon seeing Peacemaker and Born-of-Water.

A man known as *Kut-a'wi-kutz*,* got off his horse, approached, and saw Born-of-Water holding a new shovel. "What are you going to do with that?" he asked.

"Grandfather and I are going to dig a hole, father."

The children all laughed.

"Why?" *Kut-a'wi-kutz* wondered.

Born-of-Water just shrugged and glanced up at Peacemaker who was seated on a young chestnut horse.

Peacemaker narrowed his eyes and grinned. "Remember the old priest I told you about? The one called Secret Pipe? Remember what he said about becoming a chief?

Kut-a'wi-kutz had a blank look on his face.

"…The story about catching an eagle?"

"Ah, the eagle! Yes, I remember." This time it was *Kut-a'wi-kutz* who grinned. "Are you still trying to catch an eagle, father?"

Peacemaker nodded, then turned and looked at his grandson. "Hurry! Get on your horse. The day is young. We have work to do."

As grandfather and grandson rode off together, *Kut-a'wi-kutz* shook his head, turned to Cloud Wing, and said, "Still chasing a dream, isn't he, mother?"

"Always," Cloud Wing answered with pride.

---

* Hawk

And the children all giggled.

Later that evening, grandfather and grandson returned from the mountain, tired and disappointed.

"Well, did you catch an eagle?" *Kut-a'wi-kutz* asked when everyone was sitting around the campfire, eating.

"No," said Peacemaker. "We did not catch an eagle."

"But we dug a big, big hole!" cried Born-of-Water.

Everyone laughed.

Before sunup the next day, Born-of-Water and his grandfather rode off together toward the mountain and did not return until it was almost dusk. When they returned, they were tired, hungry, and frustrated. Little by little their exasperation grew and they began to question their methods, as well as themselves. That evening, while they were eating, *Kut-a'wi-kutz* asked if they had caught an eagle yet.

The answer, of course, was still the same.

The third day, grandfather and grandson woke up before sunrise and got on their horses. With them they took a large piece of meat, a fish wrapped in oil cloth, a blanket, a length of rope, and a square piece of wood, a lattice grid made of branches, tied and meshed together. The grid was about twice as big as Peacemaker was tall. On a pony drag they carried the grid and once again they rode toward the mountain with many disparaging looks from *Kut-a'wi-kutz* and others.

Once they reached the mountain, there was a pit already dug deep in the ground. Peacemaker crawled into it and while he was there he instructed his grandson to place the grid over the pit and lay more leaves and branches over the top to camouflage it.

"Good," said Peacemaker. "Now tie the fish and meat to the center of the wood—here, where my hand is." Once that was done, he told Born-of-Water to take the blanket and horses and hide among a grove of trees until he heard him call, "*Ka-coo! Ka-coo!*"

"Remember, do not harm it or kill it," reminded Peacemaker. "Now go! And do not close your eyes and fall asleep!"

So Born-of-Water hid the horses among the trees. He sat in the shade so he couldn't be seen, and there he waited. It wasn't long before he heard a call—not from his grandfather—but from a bird, a great spotted eagle whose nest was somewhere atop the mountain, upon a bluff overlooking the land below. The eagle had taken flight and was now gliding above a place called Crooked River. Back it came several minutes later. It cried out with a high-pitched chirp, swooped, and landed on the grid of branches where grandfather was hiding. The bird pecked sharply at the fish, then at the piece of meat. Each time it tried to pull the food from the grid, alternately using its beak or one or both of its powerful claws. All of a sudden, from below, a hand reached up. Through a gap it clutched at the bird's left leg.

"*Ka-coo! Ka-coo!*" Peacemaker called.

But Born-of-Water was lying down, not paying attention. Actually, he had nodded off to sleep.

Again came the call, more urgently this time.

And again, nothing happened. Born-of-Water had a fly buzzing 'round his head. He stirred, pried an eye open, swatted at the fly, and heard a desperate—"*Ka-coo! Ka-coo!*"

He bolted upright, started to run, then remembered something. He dashed behind a tree, retrieved the blanket, startling the horses in the process, and ran as fast as he could toward the pit. What he saw shocked him. The great spotted eagle, with its wings spread wide, was almost as big as him. Its head was burrowed angrily against its chest. Its left leg was being held by a hand, a bloodied hand, and the bird kept flapping its wings, scratching at the hand with its other claw, nipping at it with its beak, flapping nonstop, practically lifting the grid from the pit.

Somehow Peacemaker hung on. He yelled…shouted at Born-of-Water to hurry. Implored him. Did everything but beg.

"The blanket! I can't hold it much longer. Where are you! WHERE ARE YOU!!!"

The eagle took its beak, pecked sharply at the flesh, then raked its claw across the wrist and forearm. Blood spurted, dripping through the grid onto Peacemaker's face. Another slash or two and he had to let go. The eagle, while he knew it was strong, had an incredible amount of strength. Its legs were firm—as hard as wood—and every time it beat its wings he could feel himself being pulled upward, lifted from the pit. His head kept banging against the grid. The eagle was tenacious. As was he. Both were determined not to fail, not to give in. The cuts along his skin were deep. The pain proved it. But it wasn't just the pain from the cuts that he felt. Every time the eagle flapped its wings, it would twist its body, bounce and jerk at an angle, and he could feel his arm being twisted in ways never intended.

He had to let go.

Then he heard a shout from his grandson—"I'm coming, grandfather! I'm coming!"

There was a loud, piercing cry from above. A shriek! The eagle was in mortal fear. It flapped wildly, lashed at Peacemaker's wrist with beak and claw, and called out with alarming ferocity.

Peacemaker couldn't hold on much longer. His arm felt as if it had stretched to the point where the bones were broken. The tendons in his fingers were aching, bruised, and bleeding. Every nerve—from his fingertips to the joints in his wrists, elbow, and shoulder—was trembling in agony.

Caw!

The great bird shrieked again.

His grip loosened, then relaxed.

The struggle was over. The spotted eagle had won.

It was now free—free to fly away.

All at once there was a loud thudding from above. The grid shook, vibrated, the branches bending, shuddering. Something heavy was on top of the grid.

A shadow loomed. The grid shook again. The eagle shrieked.

Born-of-Water yelled, "I've got it! I've got it!"

The shadow withdrew. The grid was no longer shaking. Peace-maker reached up with trembling fingers, but his hand only touched air.

"Hurry, grandfather! I need you! It's big. I can't hold it much longer."

Peacemaker pushed…lifted the grid. To his amazement, Born-of-Water was sprawled on the ground, fighting to keep the eagle inside the blanket, to keep it from flying away. Peacemaker did all he could to keep from laughing. Born-of-Water was wrestling with the blanket, eyes bulging, groaning, a look of desperation in his face, while the creature kept scratching at the cloth, trying to escape.

After a few moments of tussling, of rolling around, they had the blanket fully enclosed, tied with a rope—with the great spotted eagle trapped inside alive, but apparently unhurt, for it lashed at the blanket again and again, and made sharp, chirping sounds, not as wild or as loud as shrieks, but loud enough to know it was angry. At one point the eagle ripped a hole through the cloth with its beak or claw, so they had to wrap the blanket tightly with rope, then secure it with a knot, to keep the creature from breaking free.

Once that was done, they looked at each other, smiled, and gave a weary but ecstatic cry of victory.

At the campfires that night, after everyone had eaten, after Peacemaker's hand and wrist had been wrapped in a healing cloth to stop the bleeding, *Kut-a'wi-kutz* asked with a grin, "How did you hurt your hand, father? Did you have a fight with a sharp-clawed animal? A bobcat? A wolf? An eagle perhaps?"

The children all snickered and laughed.

But Peacemaker sat quietly by the fire, waiting for the laughter to die. When it did, he nodded at Born-of-Water. Born-of-Water ran into a woods and returned a short time later, holding a blanket with a big bulge inside it. The bulge was moving, and from inside the cloth there was a muffled, bird-like chirping—

C-caw! C-caw! C-caw!

The grandchildren, children, and parents all shrank from the sound, muttering nervously to themselves and each other.

Gaping in wonder, *Kut-a'wi-kutz* stood up and said, "What sort of trick is this?"

"Trick?" said Born-of-Water, grinning. "No trick."

With a nod from his grandfather, Born-of-Water took a knife. He carefully cut the ropes, one at a time, slicing through the cords, making sure the knife didn't go too deep, while the bulge inside the blanket trembled and began to make terrible noises—

Squawk! Squawk!

Everyone retreated, mumbling nervously, unable to take their eyes off the blanket.

Born-of-Water made one last cut, lifted the rope, and stood back.

Peacemaker rose to his feet, reached out a hand, and pointed at the bulge as it squirmed inside the blanket.

"Fly!" he commanded. "Fly!"

Quickly, the blanket began to recede—until a corner flew open and the great spotted eagle, staring wild-eyed at the surrounding crowd, realized it was free.

"Fly!" Peacemaker roared.

"Fly!" cried the children.

"Fly!" everyone yelled.

With two big flaps of its wings, the eagle squawked, sprang into the air, and flew away.

Everyone stood in awe, hardly knowing what to say.

Not Peacemaker. He yawned and said, "I am tired. I think I will go to bed."

As he turned to leave, his son, *Kut-a'wi-kutz*, touched his shoulder and said, "So tell us, father. How do you catch an eagle without hurting it?"

Peacemaker thought about it for a moment and replied, "I *know*. My grandson *knows*. Now it is time for my son to *know*." And with a limp, he walked over to Cloud Wing, put an arm around her, and they disappeared into the night.

— THE END —

"*Everything the Power of the World does is done in a circle.*
The wind, in its greatest power, whirls.
Birds make their nest in circles.
The sun comes forth and goes down again in a circle.
The moon does the same and both are round.
Even the seasons form a great circle in their changing
and always come back again to where they were.
The life of a man is a circle from childhood to childhood
and so it is in everything where power moves.
Our tepees were round, like the nest of birds,
and these were always set in a circle.
The nation's hoop (is) a nest of many nests
where the Great Spirit meant for us to hatch our children.
But the Wasichus have put us in these square boxes,"

– Black Elk
from *Black Elk Speaks*

Sources

Pawnee, Blackfoot, and Cheyenne by George Bird Grinnell

Black Elk Speaks by John G. Neihardt

The Religions of the American Indians by Ake Hultkrantz

The Myths of the North American Indians by Lewis Spence

American Indian Myths and Legends by Richard Erdoes and Alfonso Ortiz

Indian Days of Long Ago by Edward S. Curtis

In the Land of the Head-Hunters by Edward S. Curtis

A Pictorial History of the American Indian by Oliver La Farge

Sacred Legacy, and the North American Indian by Edward S. Curtis

The Native Americans, the Indigenous People of North America, written and edited by contributing members of the Smithsonian Institution

To Build a Fire and Other Stories by Jack London

Call of the Wild and *White Fang* by Jack London